NEVER LOOK BACK

D1518282

Geraldine Solon

This book is a work of fiction. Names, characters, places and incidents are the product of the author's imagination or are used fictitiously. Any resemblance to actual events, locales or persons living or dead is entirely coincidental.

Jim and Cass Gronan

Chapter 1

A misty fog enveloped the sky. After grabbing her thick, wool coat and suitcase, Dana Simmons stepped down from her black Suburban SUV and drew in the cold Alaskan air. A gust of wind swept her long blond hair as she rolled her luggage to her childhood home. Tall pine trees surrounded the two-story waterfront and the old-fashioned mailbox. Opting not to knock at the front door, she headed to the back, ascended to the top of her tree house, and overlooked the frozen lakefront view.

Shutting her eyes, Dana could still hear their laughter while her father and she played hide and seek. How she wished she could run around on her father's back giggling until she was out of breath, but that wouldn't erase the twenty years she lost when her mother disappeared. Blowing out a sigh, Dana opened her eyes, climbed down the tree house, and marched to the front door.

Her father's nurse escorted her inside. "He's in the bedroom waiting for you."

Forcing a smile, Dana set the suitcase aside as she surveyed the popcorn ceiling. The old box TV blasted the famous *Wheel of Fortune* show she used to watch with her father. Dana slanted her gaze to the mustard wallpaper. Everything seemed like how it was when she left Alaska for the high-paced life in New York and L.A. Being a model was all she ever wanted—an escape from the painful reality that her mother was never coming back.

"How is he?"

The nurse's kept her eyes guarded. "He never ceases to tell me how proud he is of you."

"Thank you for taking care of him."

They shared a tight embrace.

"Happy Birthday, Dana. I'll be back in the morning."

Dana removed her UGGS and set it aside. She tied her golden blond hair in a ponytail. The smell of rubbing alcohol burned her nostrils as she entered into the dark room. Lying down with cheeks sunken, her father forced a smile. His lung cancer had deteriorated since his diagnosis two years ago.

Dana rushed to his side, tears trickling down her face. "Oh, Dad!"

Dad stroked her cheek. "Sweetie, happy birthday. Now, don't you get all depressed. You're not starving yourself today." He poked her ribs.

Dana sniffed while embracing her dad tight.

"I got your favorite cake."

She trembled. "Thank you."

A tradition they shared every year and the only time Dana could eat chocolate. With her mother gone and her father fighting for her life, who did Dana have? Sure, she had a lot of friends and an active social life, but her modeling career was taking a toll on her body. At six feet and a hundred twenty pounds, she had the ideal body, all credit to a strict diet. Not everybody could survive the cruel modeling industry. You had to pay a high price to look glamorous, when deep inside you felt like shit. A lot of fresh younger models were willing to get paid less than what she received. Her clock was ticking, and by next year, she would be over the hill for a modeling career.

Only at her father's place could Dana eat some carbs and not feel guilty. Nobody here told her that her waistline grew bigger or that she gained a pound.

"Would you help your old man up so I can sing to you?" Dad asked in his raspy voice. His blue eyes still twinkled, revealing how handsome he once was.

After adjusting the pillow behind her father's back, Dana lit the candles as her father sang Happy Birthday.

"Don't forget to make a wish."

So many things she wished for, yet everything seemed to be taken away from her. She closed her eyes then blew thirty candles.

Her father clapped so hard. "Good girl. Now you know the drill." He fingered the icing and licked his fingers.

Nodding, she lighted the candles again as they sang Happy Birthday to Dana's absent mother.

After savoring some cake, her father drifted into a deep sleep. Dana rose and lurched to the kitchen to wash the dishes.

Moments later, her father called out to her from the room. "Dana, honey..." He coughed.

"Coming, Dad." She rinsed the soap from the plate and dried the dishes, placing them on the rack before retreating to the room.

"There's something I need to tell you."

Her stomach churned as she rested on the chair beside her father's bed.

Holding her hand tight, he said, "Honey, you know I don't have much time and—"

"We don't have to talk about this," Dana cried.

His breaths turned shallow. "You can't keep running away from the past. It's a big part of you."

Dana sighed. "I didn't run away. I moved on. While you chose to..." She paused. "You *chose* to live in the past." When he didn't respond, tears flooded her cheeks. "It's been twenty years, Dad. Do you ever think Mom is out there? She probably has her own family, or she's dead."

"I will not allow you to say that about your mother." He coughed between breaths.

She bit her lip. "Let me ask you this: if Mom is alive, what kind of mother leaves her ten-year-old daughter and husband behind?"

Her father stared at the dextrose, watching every drip as if it were a timer.

Emotions unraveled before Dana as she sobbed remembering how her father had been there for her emotionally, but acted like a robot who took care of her as an obligation. "This is why I *left,* Dad. I couldn't bear to see you so unhappy, and all I needed was your love and affection."

"That's not true. I love you."

"But I needed you to share more than just a chocolate cake. I wanted you to talk to me about life, boys, and let me know how to survive." Dana covered her face.

With his frail hands, he pulled Dana toward his chest. "I'm sorry. I didn't know what to do. I hated for you to see how miserable I felt."

"You didn't have to tell me. It was painted all over your face. You became a zombie, decaying like there was nothing left." She pulled away from him, furious with herself for talking to him like this. Unwilling to face him, she approached the window. "I'm sorry, I shouldn't have said that."

Drops of snowflakes cascaded to the ground.

Before he could respond, she added, "I thought I could figure it out on my own." She paced around the room. "Which is why I kept myself busy modeling, but my career has left me emptier than I ever was. Nothing you see is real—it's all phony. All I ever wanted was a deep relationship, a normal family, and a happy home."

"Honey, listen to me. The doctor said I have a couple days, if I'm lucky."

Catching her breath, Dana rushed to his side. "No, we are fighting this disease. You can't leave me, Dad. You're all I've got."

"I've sold the house."

"What?"

"I know you're not going to live here. I only see you twice a year, three times if I'm lucky. I sold it to Michael Downey. He gave me an offer I can't refuse. The money is yours. Although you don't need it, I'm sure you will soon when you figure out what you want to do with your life. I've entrusted my attorney to give you the account details."

The world spun. She clutched her head, hoping this was just a bad dream.

"I have everything in my will." Her father opened his nightstand drawer and removed a manila envelope. "My lawyer's contact info is there. You have nothing to worry about. My memorial service has been paid, and I'm ready to go."

Dana clutched the envelope against her chest. He didn't deserve this. "I can't lose you, Dad."

"You'll be fine. Do me a favor, will you? Don't be like your old man. Go get yourself a husband, have a lot of kids, and enjoy what life gives you." He burst into laughter in between coughs. "Life is about taking risks. I know I should have moved on, but I can't change the past. But you..." He pointed to her. "You have a whole life ahead of *you*."

All Dana could do was nod.

"One last thing, please keep the albums. I want you to have them."

"Of course." They only had two family albums. Her father stopped taking photos when her mother vanished. She had more photos of her modeling career than she ever had of her childhood, yet those two albums meant more to her than she could imagine.

"I love you, Dana. I always will, my beloved daughter."

"I love you, Dad. You're the best dad in the world, you know that?"

He gave a hearty laugh and before long exhaled his last breathe.

All Dana could do was scream, "Don't go."

Chapter 2

The cathedral bells chimed as a lady dressed in a black velvet dress and high heels stepped inside the church. Her clinking heels echoed as she approached and knelt down on the back pews with head bowed. She made the sign of the cross and prayed as the priest gave the homily.

From a distance, a man wearing a black trench coat greeted the mourners. He eyed the blond woman sitting two rows in front of him then settled into the pew averting his gaze at a tall blond woman delivering her message at the podium.

"Thank you for coming here today. My father was a good citizen. He paid his bills on time, followed the law, and gave generous tithes to the church. But most of all, he was a good father, he took care of me when my mother..." She cleared her throat. "When my mother left. We honor him today for the life he lived and for the goodness in his heart. I want to thank all of you for coming here today and for remembering my father."

Waiting till everyone paid their respect, the man mounted from his seat and exited the cathedral. Reaching for his cellphone, he punched in a number and mumbled in a hushed town. "I found them—yep, mother and daughter."

***

Back in her Manhattan apartment, Dana never felt so alone. She stirred her cup of coffee while reading the morning newspaper. Despite the heater being on full blast, a cold wind managed to slip in the thin walls of her apartment at the fourteenth floor. Everything about Dana's apartment displayed a modern minimalist look with art that matched her ivory leather couch, but each time she gazed at the paintings on her wall, the more it made her mourn.

A knock startled her. *Who can it be?*

She held the door ajar as John Goodwin, her father's lawyer, greeted her with a smile.

"John, what brings you here? I thought we had finished discussing my father's will."

"I'm in town for the holidays. I forgot to give you something from your father." He rubbed his chin then pulled out a crumpled envelope from his back pocket and handed it to Dana.

"Do you want to come inside?"

"I won't stay long."

Raising her eyebrows, she opened the envelope.

"I think you should read it when I'm gone."

She glanced back at him. "Is there something you're not telling me?"

"Oh, no. Personal matters like this are between the family. I'm just the messenger who doesn't want to be part of any issues."

She nodded. "I understand. Thanks for being so helpful to us."

"You take care now, Dana, and if there's anything you need, you know where to reach me."

What I need is for my father to come home. I miss you, Dad. He died on her birthday—on her mother's birthday and twenty years after her mother had disappeared. Birthdays were supposed to be happy, but it seemed that her family was cursed.

She plucked out the letter from the envelope.

> *Dear Dana,*
> *By the time you read this, I'm gone, my ashes lost in the woods where I loved to take long walks and explore the outdoors. You know how much I love you, and being gone will not change my love for you. I'm so sorry to add this burden to you, but your mother is still alive. I never dared to look for her because I had to protect her secret that could affect you. Being the coward that I am, I chose to carry this secret to my grave. But you are different, Dana. I know you are bold and brave. I'm no longer here to protect you. Please find her, I know you will, and when you do, please tell her I never stopped loving her.*
> *I love you.*
> *Dad*

Dana read the letter more than three times. The world rotated, and she sucked in air. *A secret?*

"How could you keep this from me, Dad?" Why did she have to grow up without a mother? *How am I supposed to find Mom?*

If only her father had given her a hint.

Dana paced the room when an idea came to her. She fled to her bedroom and grasped the two family albums from her book shelf. The first picture she spotted showed her beautiful mother with long blond hair and blue eyes pushing Dana on the swing. Flipping the pages to find more clues only brought tears to her eyes as pictures of her family building a snowman and birthday parties flashed upon her.

Towards the end of the album, she spotted her mother dressed in a pink fairy costume. She remembered that night. Her parents had just arrived from a party and were arguing. "You know how I hate this place," her mother had said. "It's cold and boring, and there's nothing to do."

"Don't get so high and mighty," her father had lashed back. "This small town saved you."

"I used to be an entertainer, a good one too. I made more money in a day than you can make in a month."

Her father opened his mouth when he had caught Dana standing by the hallway. They tried to cover up the scene, but even back then, Dana understood that couples had disagreements.

She collapsed onto her bed. *What if Mom's here in New York?* Thoughts of hiring a private detective dawned on her, but she brushed it aside. Pacing around her bedroom, she wondered where would her mom be. *I need to start somewhere. If Mom is like me, she would love The Big Apple.*

Outside the window, gray clouds nestled. People flocked the streets, preparing for the Christmas holidays, but all she could think about was finding her mother. She flipped through the pages of a magazine that listed a variety of performances, but she didn't know if her mother was a magician, dancer, singer, gymnast, or comedian. Would Dana even recognize her mother?

Grabbing her cell phone, she punched in Rob's phone number. Rob wasn't only her agent and photographer—he was her best friend.

"How's my favorite girl?" Rob's cheerful voice brought back her high spirits.

"I don't think I can go back to work yet."

"I understand you're grieving. Maybe we can have lunch soon. Are you still in Alaska?"

"Nope, I'm back home."

"And you never called?" He lowered his voice. "Don't tell me you're trying to drown your emotions. You know that's not very smart of you."

"No, nothing like that. I'm trying to figure out how to find my mother."

There was a long pause. "Your mother? Isn't she—"

"She vanished. My father's lawyer just delivered a letter where Dad confessed that Mom's still alive."

"What? He never told you?"

"He said he was trying to protect me. If you had met my father, you would have understood he was a peacemaker." Deep inside, Dana wished he'd told her. Whatever his reasons were, she couldn't understand why he didn't.

"I'm so sorry, but this doesn't make sense. Why didn't he look for her?"

"Long story. It's all very confusing for me, but I have to look for her. I have a feeling she's here— I hope she is." She drew in a breath.

Rob sighed. "You can always hire a private detective."

Dana licked her lips. "I thought of that, but I prefer to do this myself."

"I'm worried about you. You have to be careful. You're an international model, and people can take advantage of you."

"Don't you worry about me. I know how to take care of myself. Besides, I have my perfect disguise," Dana said.

"I hear you. You have your wigs, hat, and sunglasses, right?"

"You know me so well."

"Does this mean you won't be coming back to work?"

"I don't know how long this will take. I'm sorry if I have to cancel some of my projects."

"You'll be missing lots of opportunities."

"I know, Rob, but she's still my mother and it involves my life. I hope you understand my priorities."

"Of course I do. I miss my favorite girl." Rob's tender tone comforted her.

Silence crossed between them. Rob often joked that if they didn't meet anyone special, they should just get married. She could still taste the drunken kiss they shared two years ago at a New Year's Eve party. She'd always have a soft spot for Rob.

"You'll find twenty-year-olds who can do a better job than me."

"Not everybody has that sweet smile like you."

A grin played on her lips. "Thanks for cheering me up. You're a true friend."

"I'm your evil twin," he teased.

"Yeah, yeah. Anyway, I gotta go."

"Are you coming for the holiday dinner tonight?"

"Sorry," Dana said, "I don't think I'm in any mood to celebrate, but I'll be in touch."

"You hang in there. I'm here for you. Merry Christmas, my friend, and let's get together before the New Year."

"Merry Christmas."

Dana hung up and clutched her purse. Fingering her locket necklace, she eyed her family photo. "I'm going to find you, Mom." She slipped into her boots, exited her apartment, and headed for the elevator. Perhaps a walk in Central park would help her clear her head. It felt nice to be alone, with nobody pressuring her to change clothes for the runway.

"Ms. Simmons, this came in for you this morning." A bellboy handed her a medium-sized box.

"Thank you." She removed the card and read it.

> *Dear Dana,*
> *Have you ever dreamed of*
> *finding someone or something that*
> *you thought you could never have?*
> *Well, now's your chance.*
> *Happy Holidays.*

Heart pounding, Dana glanced around. *Is this a joke?*

"Do you know who sent this?" she asked the bellboy.

"I was in the bathroom and noticed it was here when I came back."

Dana examined the tag labeled *Ginny's Delights*. Since when would someone send her a fruitcake for Christmas?

"Can I leave this here? I'll pick it up when I come back."

"Sure." The bellboy tucked it beneath the counter. "Have a nice day."

"Thank you."

She took a morning stroll. People walked past her and didn't recognize her. Living in Manhattan made her used to walking. The Christmas songs depressed her. All she wanted to do was to clear her head and find answers.

Chapter 3

A lady fingered the shawl wrapped around her neck as she crossed the street. A cab driver screeched in front of her and flipped her off. She entered the church and stepped inside the confession box. Kneeling down, she made the sign of the cross.

"What can I do for you?"

"Father... I can't keep hiding."

"What are you hiding from?"

The woman lit a cigarette and took a puff.

"You can't smoke here."

"I've wasted twenty years of my life." She wept. "I've hurt my family."

"God always gives us hope."

"I can never look back and erase what I did, but today I saw how beautiful my daughter has become and I know she deserves the truth."

The door yanked open and a pair of hands covered her mouth. Then all she saw was black.

***

Crossing the street at Madison Square, Dana searched for a good place to have lunch. Her walk had turned into an hour-long trek, and she felt dehydrated and hungry. Stomach growling, Dana dug into her purse.

A hand clung to her arm. Cigarette smoke blocked her view.

"Good afternoon, Dana Simmons."

Dana took a step back. Her disguise had failed her. The man stood about four inches shorter than her. Soft curls slightly covered his face, and sunglasses concealed his eyes. "I'm not working if it's an autograph that you want."

He gave a slight grin, exposing his yellow teeth, and pulled down the zipper of his leather jacket down.

Dana eyed the gun tucked between his high-waisted jeans above his beer belly. She tried to remain calm as her palms began to moisten. People were strolling around unaware of what was going on. As she stood there, all Dana could hear was her father's words, *Find her.* Now drenched from nerves, Dana shivered. Nobody knew where she went today. With her father gone, who will come looking for her? No time to think. If she ran, where would she go?

Bidding for time to come up with a plan, she straightened her shoulders and gave off an air of indifference as best she could. "What do you want from me?

"I suggest you come with me."

A Cadillac pulled up to the curb. A man popped out of the car and pushed Dana toward it.

Dana opened her mouth to scream when the man pointed the gun at her back. "I will shoot you."

"Get off me."

He covered her mouth.

The man with the gun studied her from head to toe. "You're more beautiful in person. You don't need much make-up to show that radiant beauty." He shoved her inside the back seat and towards the driver, he demanded. "Drive."

The red-head driver locked the door and sped away.

Dana tried to open the door, but laughter erupted from the man holding the gun. She tucked her hands underneath her thighs studying the leather seats and where the driver was taking them. Traffic was from bumper to bumper, but she couldn't escape. And Dana could easily jump out and escape but she knew better not too.

The man gave a hoarse laugh. "Poor Dana, lonely as can be."

"You know nothing about me!" She yelled.

He pulled her cashmere scarf. "You better pay attention to me, because I know everything about you that there is to know."

Dana tugged her scarf from him. "Where are you taking me?"

His upper lip curled back in a snarl. "You're not allowed to ask any questions."

Dana rubbed her hand against the leather seat, mapping out her plan to escape. The redheaded driver swerved to the freeway, leaving the city of New York heading north. He still hadn't spoken yet.

The man beside her hummed a tune that would drive birds away. His raspy voice sent a dull ache to her ears. He removed his jacket, revealing a tattoo of a dagger and skull on his arm.

She made a mental note to remember this.

"I need to use the bathroom," she said.

He forced a smile. "Lady, that's the oldest trick in the book."

Dana shook her head. "I haven't eaten anything since last night, and I'm getting lightheaded."

He waved his gun around. "Listen, you prima donna, don't think you can order me around like you do with your staff. I'm in charge now."

"I'm still a human being." She attempted to open the window. No luck. Locked.

"Don't even think of escaping." He narrowed his eyes. "You're my prisoner now." He burst into laughter reminding her of the brutal auditions she had when she first started modeling.

Dana stared outside the window at the huge array of colonial houses. Taking a deep breath, she pretended to be a suburban mom grilling steaks on a warm summer afternoon for her husband and kids.

The man nudged her roughly on her arm. "We're here."

The man clutched her arm and forced her out of the car, the gun pressing against her back. The red-head driver trails behind them. Marching, they approached an empty driveway of the only house in the area. This was a two-story smaller house with no garden up front.

The man clung Dana to him while they entered the house. The living room was empty with no furniture except for the dust and cobwebs in the corner. The marble floors shone seeming untouched by shoes. He forced Dana to the kitchen where there were bar stools and a breakfast nook.

A half-empty open box of donuts rested on the counter. "Eat."

Dana rolled her eyes.

The man pushed her to the barstool. "I said eat." When she refused, his mouth carved into a grin. He pressed a strawberry glazed donut into her mouth.

She spat it out directly at his face.

He slapped her face knocking her off to the ground.

"You asshole!" Rising from the floor, she dashed and elbowed him. Kicking her leg, she stumbled to the floor as he cocked his gun to her head.

"I'm going to blow your brains out."

Gasping for breath, she realized she had no choice but to obey Skully. Yes, that's the nickname she gave him, She was trapped in an abandon house, miles away from civilization, a gun pointed at her.

Her cell phone rang.

Skully jolted and snatched her purse. "You ain't answering that."

"Do you have to take everything away from me?"

"I told you. I'm in charge."

A knot formed in her stomach. *What if he kills me? God forbid, what have I gotten myself into?* If only her father didn't write that letter. Maybe her mother was better served as a memory… What you don't know can't hurt you.

She sat down on the bar stool trying to figure out how she could escape.

"You want to know why you're here?"

Her ears perked up but how could she trust him.

Skully bent down to stroke her hair bringing it closer to his nostrils. "Hmm. I love the smell of lavender mixed with lime."

She tilted her head away from him.

He only held her closer and whispered in her ear, "I know where your mother is."

Swallowing hard, she said, voice low, "My mom passed away years ago."

He kicked the chair opposite where she sat and gave that long admonishing laugh of his. "Liar."

She rose from her chair and threw the box of donuts at his face. "You freak!"

Skully's face flushed with rage like he was ready to pounce at her. "Bitch."

Dana dropped down to her knees and wept. The marble floors didn't cool the mixed emotions she felt inside. There was no more turning back. Not only was her mother alive—something that up until now, she still hadn't quite accepted—her mother was in danger. They both were, and it would be up to Dana to save her.

"You're never getting out of here." Skully stormed out of the kitchen, and the last thing she heard was the door bang and switching of the lock.

Chapter 4

FBI Agent Kerry Wayne stared at the mishmash stack of folders on his office desk. Each folder contained data of four missing women in the last year in Manhattan alone.

He adjusted the picture frame of his two daughters and ex-wife, glad that they were safe. He was long overdue for a vacation to visit them in Aspen.

His partner, Agent Felicia Raymond, a skinny, flat-chested woman, kept her eyes glued to a corkboard connecting the locations and dates when the victims disappeared while phones rang off the hook.

"This doesn't make sense," Felicia said.

"What doesn't?" He glanced at her.

"These four women, except for Maria Garcia were last seen near the Empire State building. Someone claimed they spotted Maria at the airport in Queens."

Kerry shrugged. "Could be a lookalike, who knows."

"Yes, but all the rest are from out of state. Maria has lived in Manhattan all her life."

Kerry rubbed his chin. Her newbie-ness was showing—thorough and overly eager. "Maybe she wanted to escape the cold winters. Some missing persons prefer to erase their past and start anew."

"I don't know about you, but I'm starting to think there's a syndicate out there profiling women who are between twenty-eight and twenty-nine years old."

Fear crawled inside him. His twins, who were tall and skinny like them, were now that age, and God forbid that should happen to them.

Felicia nudged him and opened a folder on his desk. "Did you hear what I said?"

"Sorry. Maybe he narrowed his search to that age group. We need to know more about these women—their hobbies, jobs and why he would target them."

"How do you know it's a he?" She tossed the folders onto his desk. "These women are six feet tall."

Kerry glanced at the folders then back at Felicia. "Okay, Felicia, looks like you don't need a partner like me."

She folded her arms and cocked her head to the side. "Are you kidding me? Who do you think will protect me from the wackos out there?" She circled her way back to her desk across him.

He tossed her a sandwich from his chair. "I've got your back."

***

Dana screamed until her lungs burned, but all she heard was her echo. She dashed in each room and opened the closets and found nothing. She threw a barstool against the window, but the panes didn't shatter. Dana only spotted empty land. "Fuck!"

She zipped up her sweater and tried to adjust the temperature to seventy five degrees in the living room. It was busted. *Damn it!*

Dana continued exploring the three-bedroom house. "There's gotta be something here."

Other than an uncompleted room with blank walls and no closets and the floor not marble like the rest of the house, she found nothing.

She opened the medicine cabinet in the bathroom. Bare. Darting back to the kitchen, she spied the box of donuts on the floor and the Mountain Dew on the counter. Her stomach growled, but all she could focus on was escape.

Dana ransacked the drawers. The top one was empty. Same with the second. Each time she opened the drawers, her frustration grew. "This is insane."

She opened the last drawer. Lo and behold, she caught a glimpse of a screwdriver gleaming in front of her eyes. Her heart galloped. Beneath is sat a business card for Ginny's Delights.

"Oh my God. The fruitcake."

The front door creaked.

Hands shaking, she tucked the screwdriver and business card inside her sweater and plopped herself on the bar stool.

Skully popped in with a paper bag. "Brought you some food." He removed the hot dogs and chips then eyed the box of donuts. "You didn't eat?"

Dana bit her lower lip. "Um, I wasn't hungry."

He slapped her face. "Didn't your mother teach you to eat what's on the table?"

She laid a hand on her cheek.

Skully shoved a hot dog toward her mouth. "Eat."

Dana spat the hotdog on the countertop. *Disgusting!* She dug into her pocket and reached for the screwdriver.

Skully slapped her again. "What is wrong with you?"

Dana studied his features contemplating which eyeball she could poke. She had to plan this well. He wore the same leather jacket and his gun must have been tucked inside his pocket. If only she could get a hold of it.

"What are you looking at?"

She lowered her gaze to his pockets. If she jabbed his eye and missed, would he have time to grab his gun before she got to the door?

"Oh, I know. You're one of those freaks. What do you call them? Vegans?" He burst into a raspy laugh. "Well, guess what, you better eat this damn hot dog, or I'm going to thrust it down your throat."

Dana drew in a shaky breath. The last time she ever ate a hot dog was before her modeling days. She'd been a vegan as far as she remembered and looking at meat disgusted her. Donuts, chips, and Mountain Dew were never on her grocery list. Mornings would be a vegetable or fruit smoothie. Each time she had a photo shoot, she would munch on carrots or broccoli for a meal.

She grabbed the hotdog and took a bite while closing her eyes.

Skully laughed so hard Dana wanted to punch him on the nose.

To force the sandwich down, she tried to imagine she was eating a vegan one, like the kind she made when she could have carbs.

Skully opened the bag of potato chips and popped a piece in his mouth. "I don't know how you vegans ever enjoy. Life is to be savored."

Ignorant motherfucker!

Munching away, Skully sat on top of the counter. After savoring a big gulp of soda, Skully released a nasty burp.

Oh, how she hated him.

After eating the meal, she wiped her mouth with a napkin and stifled the urge to throw up. She straightened her shoulders. "That wasn't so bad." If Skully thought he was going to manipulate her, he was mistaken. "So, what are our plans for today?"

He laughed, exposing the chips glued onto his teeth. "You think this is a game?"

"You kidnapped me and leave me in an abandoned house. You sure have a plan, don't you?"

Skully crumpled the paper bag and tossed it at Dana's face. She ducked, and it tumbled to the floor. Dana broke into a grin.

Pushing her against the wall, Skully raised his eyebrows. "You think that's funny, huh? I make the rules, not you."

His smelly breath entered her lungs. She was ready to dodge him with the screwdriver, but decided otherwise needing to dig deeper.

Skully let go of her shirt and washed his hands in the sink.

"All I'm saying is if I'm going to stay here, I'll need a change of clothes and toiletries and, there's no bed for me to sleep in."

He smirked.

"What do you want from me, anyway? If it's money, I don't have much. If you're th—"

"You don't stop yakking, do you? Why don't you just do what you do best on the catwalk or strike a pose? That's all you really are, a pretty face with nothing inside."

Dana glared at him as blood rose to her head. She knew better than to explode. He had to want exactly that with what he was spouting. So, she gave him the brightest smile and took off her sweater to do the catwalk. "Sure, if that's what you want."

His eyes gleamed in delight as he watched her walk from the kitchen to the living room and back. Dana did her signature pose, swaying her hips from side to side as she marched back and forth. She pretended there was an audience while she fondled her hair and smiled.

When it was over, he clapped his hands. "Wow. You are good."

Flushed cheeks, Dana smiled. "Thank you." With his size, the screwdriver might be better as a last resort. Maybe she'd have a better chance of getting out of here if he trusted her, if she used her charm and followed his orders.

Grabbing the box of donuts, she indulged herself and moaned. "Wow! How did you know glazed donuts were my favorite?"

He jerked back. "But I thought you were a vegan?"

She patted him on the shoulder like an old friend. "Silly. You think models like me don't have cravings like these? Like you said, vegans are boring and I like to have fun sometimes."

He blinked his eyes. "What do you want me to bring you next time?"

Swallowing hard, Dana hoped there would be no next time. "I dunno, maybe a blanket, some clothes. How about a book? It gets lonely here, you know." She covered herself with the sweater.

"Tell you what. If you continue to smile at me and do the catwalk, I'll bring you anything you want."

Dana raised her eyebrows. "Anything?" She leaned closer. "You still haven't told me your name. You know everything about me, but I don't know anything about you."

Skully blushed then glanced at his watch. "Time to go. Will be back tomorrow."

"You're going to leave me here alone?"

Skully rose and grabbed the trash. "What do you think, my lady, I would sleep here beside you?"

"But there's no bed and the heater doesn't work. You can't just leave me here."

"Have a good evening, Dana." Skully broke into a sprint and left, the sound of the door locking piercing the silence.

Darkness crept in, and Dana had never felt so alone.

Chapter 5

Daylight spilled inside the window. She spent the whole evening trying to unscrew the door knob only to find out there were other locks she couldn't unfasten from the inside.

Dana rose from the kitchen floor and went to the sink to wash her face. She removed the business card from her pocket and read the address. A pastry shop on Madison Avenue, two blocks from her apartment. Why was the card here? And right after someone, maybe her mother, sent her a fruitcake from there. *Is this where Mom works?*

Stroking her locket kept her from feeling isolated. "Help!!!"

Still no signs of Skully. Dana peered outside the window and watched the snowflakes. Three days until Christmas. Would Rob come looking for her?

Dana stared at the hot dog and donuts and pushed it aside. Skully was surely playing games with her and just when she thought she had won him. She brushed back her hair, the oil making her feel filthy.

She lay on the floor and closed her eyes and her thoughts shifted to the day before her mother disappeared.

Her mother had braided Dana's hair that evening.

"Mommy, I'm going to be ten tomorrow."

"Yes, and we're going to celebrate our birthdays in style." She watched her mother comb her long blond hair before applying lipstick.

"What are we going to do?"

"It's a surprise. I promise to make it special."

Snow hit the windowpane and jolted Dana back to reality. She rose and gazed outside to witness a snowstorm. Shivering, she checked the heater, but still no luck.

"Damn it." Maybe running back and forth from the living room to the kitchen to the bedrooms would keep her warm. For the next hour, Dana felt the adrenalin rush upon her as she broke into a sweat. Beads of moisture leaked down her nape. She felt good until she realized she had no food except for the hotdog and donuts.

Dana slowed down her pace and took deep breaths. She strode to the bathroom and removed her clothes. Maybe a shower was what she needed to let her feel fresh. As the water dripped down her body, Dana imagined she was lathering her hair with shampoo and her body with soap.

***

Rob Hanson left his sixth voicemail for Dana. "Why aren't you picking up? Did you receive my messages? The producer is in town and wants to do a holiday shoot. You would be perfect for this role." He exhaled. "I can't believe you'll pass on this."

He threw his phone inside his black leather messenger bag, grabbed his keys, and left his apartment. *If Dana's not picking up, I'll come and see her myself.*

Rob run his fingers through his soft wavy hair as he crossed the street. The wind blew against his cheek, and snow curled to the ground. Moments later, he arrived at Dana's apartment.

A familiar doorman greeted him. "Good day. Are you here to see Ms. Simmons?"

Rob smiled. "Yes."

He removed something from the mailbox and handed a boxed fruitcake to Rob. "She left this. Hope you don't mind taking it to her."

"Sure."

Rob entered the elevator and whistled as he pressed the fourteenth floor. He sniffed the plastic and inhaled extracts of cinnamon and cranberry.

The elevator opened. Rob bounced out and rushed to Dana's apartment. He knocked. No answer. Knocked again, still no answer. *Where are you?* He pulled out a piece of paper from his notepad and wrote "call me" in bold letters. Signing his name, Rob tucked the note underneath her door and decided to bring the fruitcake with him.

***

Nightfall came and still no Skully. Dana guarded the window and kicked the wall again and again. *I can't believe Skully has forgotten me.* She paced around the room trying to find an escape.

Banging her hands against the wall, she yelled. Dana closed her eyes and as she drifted into a deep sleep, Dana dreamt of her father playing hide and seek with her. She sought solace in her favorite hiding place, the tree house.

"Dana, I know where you are."

Giggling in between breaths, Dana whispered, "You're never going to find me here."

"Dana." His voice drew nearer.

Suddenly, she heard another voice—a woman.

Dana peered from the tree house to get a closer look and saw her mother smiling at her, blue eyes dancing. "Mom?"

The door flung open and yanked Dana from her deep sleep. The redheaded driver stood in the doorway, carrying a huge bag and a mattress.

She bolted right up. "What are you doing here? Where's Skully?"

He furrowed his eyebrows.

"I mean, the other guy, what's his name."

He unloaded a blanket and contents from an overnight bag. "Do you want me to take this to your room?"

He finally spoke. "My room?" She shrugged. No way she was making this her home. She had purposely slept in the living room so she'd be closer to the door. "You can lay it down here."

"I brought you clothes." He studied her body. "Size zero, I presume?"

She didn't flinch. "Thanks." Dana took the pajamas, toiletries, and underwear from him.

He laid food on the kitchen counter as she followed him. "You must be hungry. I have avocado rolls, hot miso soup, and udon noodles."

She grabbed the soup. "How can you guys just leave me here with nothing? The damn heater doesn't work, and I'm not only filthy, I'm starving."

He pushed the rolls toward her and watched as she munched away.

"Please, you seem like a nice guy who got dragged to do this dirty job. Can you at least tell me what I'm doing here? Or what you want from me?"

He removed his watch and washed his hands on the sink.

Dana munched her sixth avocado roll then stopped. Just as a model could control what she ate, she knew better than to eat more. She set the food aside.

"You should try the noodles."

She smiled. "I'll save it for tomorrow."

***

Rob gritted his teeth at the police station. Two hours had passed and nobody seemed to be giving importance to him. Phones rang off the hook, and the police officer he was talking to kept glancing from left to right as prostitutes walked in.

"For the third time, I'm telling you my friend doesn't just ran off like that. It's been three days since she left her apartment, and I would like to file for a missing report."

The police officer jotted notes. "Doesn't she have any family? It's the holidays, you know."

"Didn't you hear what I told you earlier? Her father just died." Rob paused then grabbed his jacket disgusted by the lack of competence. "You know what, forget it. You're not being very helpful." Rob stormed out of the office.

Back on the street, Rob stopped to buy a cigarette. He lit one and closed his eyes. So what if he had quit a couple of months ago. He needed one now. None of Dana's friends knew where she was. This was very unlike Dana to walk away when projects were lined up for her. A cold shiver ran through his spine as he recalled what Dana had said to him about her mother.

Tossing his cigarette, Rob flagged down a cab and climbed in. "East Seventy-Third Street."

The Indian cab driver drove away.

Rob gazed at the traffic jam from his window. "Is there any way you can go faster?"

The driver grinned. "What's the matter with you people? Always in a hurry."

Rob sighed. He needed to get back to Dana's apartment. If the police were not going to help, he needed to find her himself.

Half a hour later, the cab dropped him off the curb and Rob handed him folded bills. "Keep the change."

The grin on the driver's face morphed into a huge smile.

Rob dashed inside the building. The same doorman greeted him. "Listen, I need your help."

The doorman nodded. "What can I do for you?"

Rob caught his breath. "When was the last time you saw Dana?"

The doorman looked above the ceiling. "Hmm, it must have been that day I told her about the fruitcake. Like three days ago."

"That's it. She took off and hasn't come back."

"Do you think she's with a friend or out of town?"

Rob shook his head. "Did anyone aside from me come looking for her?"

The doorman pulled out the logbook. "Let me check." He flipped the pages. "Oh, yes, there was somebody by the name of John Goodwin who came to see her that morning. Never seen him before."

"Goodwin? Doesn't ring a bell."

"Is everything all right? You don't suppose Ms. Simmons—"

"I don't know. You guys have cameras, right? Do you think I can look at the tapes?"

The doorman straightened his shoulders. "Mister…" He cleared his throat.

"Hanson."

"Mr. Hanson, I don't know what your business is with Ms. Simmons, but I won't be able to assist you. May I suggest you speak to my manager?" He's not here now but here's his business card.

"Thank you."

"You're welcome."

Rob exited the building and took the longer route back to his apartment to give him time to collect his thoughts.

Once he reached home, Rob heated the teapot and plopped himself on the couch. He opened his laptop and browsed photos he had taken of Dana before she left for Alaska. Her smile made his heart leap. Oh how he missed her. Dana was his favorite model. So down-to-earth and funny and easy going…

Rob poured the hot water into his mug, added a tea bag, then stirred. *Where could she be?* He smelled traces of cinnamon and remembered the fruitcake on the table. "Shit."

Jotting down the address from the dessert's lid, Rob grabbed his keys and raced out the door, without having even one sip of tea.

Twenty minutes later, Rob studied Ginny's Delights pastry shop. The bright neon lights and light brown tables displayed a modern twist. The place looked like a favorite hangout among young women. He glanced at the selections.

A clerk with strawberry blond hair smiled at him. "Want to try our special? Fruitcake for the holidays."

Rob pointed to the mousse. "I'm more of a chocolate kinda guy."

She punched in the cash register. "You made the right choice. That's three dollars."

He dug in his pocket, pulled out dollar bills, and handed them to her.

"How long has this place been here?" He studied the surroundings noticing more women than men.

She sliced the mousse and put it on a plate. "Family business." Tying her hair in a bow, she added. "Been here for as long as I can remember."

Taking the tray from her, he asked, "Now why does that sound so bad?"

Pursing her lips, she said, "Trust me, when all you see is sugar every day, you'd wanna shift to salt."

Rob nodded. "Nice one."

She winked.

He headed to the corner table and indulged in his chocolate mousse. Another young lady who looked like the woman's sister brought a batch of cupcakes to the table next to his He could barely hear voices from the back. Maybe he would come again tomorrow and pretend to be working on his projects. The lady seemed nice, and she might be able to help him. After all, this was his only lead.

Chapter 6

When the driver fled that evening, he left behind his watch on the counter, whether intentionally or not, she thanked God he did and it had a date listed. December twenty-third. At least she had clean clothes and blankets. The first thing she did was wash her hair. She stayed in the shower as long as she could imagine allowing the strong water pressure to warm her body. Mr. redhead had been kind enough to bring her lotion and a razor. All these special treatment meant a lot to her. But then she pinched herself. She couldn't let her guard down. They obviously wanted something from her.

Dana dried her hair with the towel and gazed at her reflection in the mirror. Pale and sunken cheeks stared back at her. *Will I ever get out of here?*

***

"You're here again," the lady at the pastry shop greeted Rob the next afternoon as he sat at the same table working on his laptop.

The café was empty, hopefully the perfect time to gather information and clues. He nodded. "Yeah, thought I'd try the mango parfait for a change."

"Stacy Kestav." She offered her name as she leaned closer to check the screen. "Wow, did you take these photos?"

"Rob." He extended his hand. "Yup."

Her eyes glimmered. "You're an amazing photographer. I've never seen such beautiful work."

Rob grinned. Although Stacy wasn't tall or thin like a model, she had a refreshing face with light freckles on the bridge of her nose. Her green eyes lit up when she smiled, and her strawberry blond hair looked smooth and silky. She reminded him of a younger Dana when he met her almost a decade ago. "Thank you. Perhaps I can take photos of you as well."

Stacy titled her head to the side. "Oh, but I'm no match to those models." She covered her face.

"Trust me, this…" He pointed to the screen. "It's all airbrush, make up, and proper lighting. You have natural beauty."

Stacy giggled.

A short feisty looking woman from the back appeared. She settled her cold stern eyes on Rob. "Stacy. I've been calling you," she said in a harsh Russian accent.

Stacy pursed her lips. "I'm sorry, just give me a minute." She nodded to Rob, who slipped her a business card.

"Call me." To the woman, he said, "I would love to take photos of your pastries. I'm a photographer." He rose from his seat.

The woman nodded. "Not, today, very busy baking. You make appointment some other time."

Rob nodded. "Okay." He sat back on his chair and continued to answer emails from model applicants. An hour had gone by as the ring from his cell phone jolted him. "This is Rob."

"Mr. Hanson, this is Arnold, the doorman from Ms. Simmons' apartment."

Rob moved the phone to his left ear. "Yes, I hear you."

"I think you need to come over if you can. I told my manager—"

"I'll be there in a few." Rob shut his laptop, put on his jacket, and exited the café. From the corner of his eye, he saw Stacy watch him leave.

Rob brisked through the crowd and crossed the street. A car honked at him, but he didn't slow down. He entered the building. Arnold stood beside a tall man with salt-and-pepper hair.

"Mr. Hanson, I'm glad you came," Arnold said. "I'd like to introduce you to the building manager, Mr. Philip Doyle."

"Please to meet you." Philip extended his hand. "Arnold tells me you're a good friend of Ms. Simmons."

"Yes." Rob gripped his hand. "Has she returned yet?"

Philip shook his head. "I'm afraid not, I've already spoken to the police about this and they seem to stonewall me. Since Dana has been a long-time resident of the Palisades, I'd be happy to go over the videotapes with you."

"Oh, thank God." Rob boxed his hand in the air.

Leaving Arnold behind, Philip led Rob to the back room where two TV monitors were displayed. They sat beside each other as Philip rewound the tape to December nineteenth. "Here's Dana leaving the building. You'll see moments later when she returns with a shopping bag." He fast-forwarded the tape. "Here's the man who came in for her."

Rob leaned to get a closer look. "The Goodwin guy, right?"

"Yes, and here's Dana coming down minutes after he left. You see her chatting with Arnold where he hands her a box. She reads it and looks like she tells him to hang on to it. That's the last time we saw her. She hasn't returned ever since. We checked her mail, but it's mostly junk."

Rob folded his arms. "She doesn't even have a luggage or overnight bag. What time was this?"

Philip glanced at the screen. "Morning, around a quarter after ten."

"And we don't have footage of the delivery person from Ginny's Delights."

Philip rewound the videos and replayed them. "Nothing."

"It's very unlike Dana to go away like that. She just lost her father to lung cancer and had recently arrived from Alaska. I know she's grieving but…"

"And you've spoken to the police?" Philip rose from his seat.

"Yes, but they're useless," Rob sighed

"You can file a missing person's report. It's more than forty-eight hours."

"You're right, but lucky if I get somebody to help me during Christmas Eve."

"That's all we have to show you."

***

Rob sat across from the desk of the same officer he spoke to the last time. "I'm telling you, Officer Jones, my friend doesn't work that way. I checked the video tapes at the apartment building, and she left on December twenty at a quarter after ten in the morning with no suitcase."

Officer Jones crossed his legs. "And why are you doing my job?"

"Damn it! I came here the other day, and you dismissed my pleas." He contemplated if he should tell them about the letter Dana received from her father, but decided against it. "The law says that I can file a missing report if it's more than–"

"That's correct." Officer Jones cut him off then eyed the clock.

Rob banged his hand on the table. "Oh, no, no, no, don't you look at the clock. I know you're thinking about getting back to your family for Christmas Eve, but do you realize that Dana could be out there suffering?"

Officer Jones straightened his shoulders. "All right, fill this out and I will file the report, but you need to cooperate with us and let us do the investigation." He handed him forms. "A detective will be assigned to this case. He will call you."

Rob filled out the forms and placed them on the desk. "I'm not moving until you assure me a detective will call me tonight."

Officer Jones glanced at the forms. "Hey, does she have a list of relatives we can call?"

Rob frowned. "She has a distant aunt in Arizona. She doesn't have any cousins that I know off. She's the only child. I called a bunch of her friends. None of them have heard from Dana."

"Write their numbers down."

Rob checked his iPhone and jotted the information down.

Officer Jones bit his lip. "I hate to tell you, but we've seen this case numerous times. Woman disappears, and later on, we discover she took a vacation to some exotic paradise." He leaned forward. "Didn't you say she's a model? She most likely wants some peace and quiet from all the cameras."

Rob didn't budge. "That's still no excuse. I stand my ground."

"You don't stop, do you? Give me your card. He will call you. In the meantime, get out of here and have some Christmas cheer."

Rob gave him a dirty look.

"We'll be in touch."

Chapter 7

Rob bid goodbye to the last model in his studio and rushed upstairs. It was Christmas Eve, and he needed to drive to his parents' house in New Jersey. His mother wouldn't forgive him if he arrived late. His two brothers and their families would be there too. He loved living in New York where he had the option of having his work studio and living premises above in one loft, but at times he had to learn to balance work and home. As he shut the studio lights, a knock sounded at the door. Rob glanced at his watch, and his stomach growled. It had been hours since he last ate. Hesitating, he opened the door, taken aback to see Stacy standing outside wrapped in a fur coat with a smile plastered on her face.

"Hi."

"What a surprise!"

"Um." She bit her lip. "I hope it's not too late, but I feel I owe you an apology for what happened earlier today. I won't stay long. I know it's Christmas."

Rob swung the door open. "Come in. No need to apologize, I understand."

"My mother doesn't like the idea of me chatting with customers."

"So I gathered."

Stacy stepped inside and studied his loft. Swirling around the white open space, she beamed. "Wow. What an amazing place you have here." She laid her purse on the couch and sat down.

He shut the door behind him and sat on the couch. "Can I offer you a drink? Red wine?"

"Sure."

Rob headed for the kitchen and poured two glasses then strode back to the couch. "So tell me, what do you do aside from managing your family business?" He handed her a glass.

Crossing her legs, Stacy said. "I love going to museums. I'm actually leaving."

"Leaving?"

"If I stay here any longer, I won't be able to make a life of my own. I'm going to Paris in March."

"Hmm. Paris?"

"I know, something different, right?" She took a sip. "I want to explore the city, learn French, and who knows? Maybe make a life there."

"That's great."

Stacy set the glass on the coffee table and removed her coat. Rob's eyes opened wide as she bared her flawless naked body. She had curves in the right places and well-defined breasts with a sunflower tattoo on her belly button. Not that he hadn't seen models nude before. He just hadn't expected Stacy to approach him this way.

She winked. "I thought I'd take your offer."

He swallowed hard. "Right."

Like a professional, Rob approached the camera and fitted the lens then played with the lights.

Stacy lay on the floor, her head leaning toward the left as Rob snapped away. *She's a natural.*

Thoughts of Dana clamored upon him, and he felt guilty admiring Stacy. Dana was always on his mind. He never had the courage to tell her how he felt, but deep inside, he knew Dana was aware of this.

Temptation tugged his inside as Stacy played with different poses.

"It's a wrap," Rob said. "Congratulations, you look wonderful."

The sudden pinkness of her cheeks only enhanced her natural beauty. "Can I see?"

Rob shook his head. "I never show the raw pictures. I'll mail you copies."

Approaching him, she traced her finger on his jaw. "You don't have to mail the photos. I'd love to see you again."

Stacy leaned closer and pressed her lips on his. With eyes shut, Rob couldn't resist her soft lips. He found himself melting in her kisses and still couldn't believe Stacy would do this. At the pastry shop, Stacy appeared like a school girl, but she wasted no time starting to undress Rob.

Rob pulled away to catch his breath. "Wait a minute. I'm not sure this is right. I hardly know you."

She clasped her hand against his and brought it to cup her breast. "We can talk later. You don't want to lose the momentum."

Closing his eyes, he let Stacy take the lead as she finished undressing him. She was powerful and maneuvered ever inch of his body with her tongue. Lost in her touch, Rob's desire grew as he laid her down and thrust inside her. She closed her eyes and moaned as he licked her breasts. Stacy tasted like honey, her body fresh like the morning dew. Her thighs locked around his buttocks as he rocked inside her. When they both released, Rob collapsed beside her. Holding her tight, Rob traced her jaw with his fingers and kissed her.

Moments later, Stacy grabbed her coat and kissed him goodbye. "Happy holidays, Rob."

The clicking of her heels and she was gone. Rob covered his face. This wasn't the first time a client seduced him after a pictorial, but he had broken his golden rule about not sleeping with clients. He never believed in casual sex. However, Stacy had caught him off guard. He couldn't deny his attraction, yet everything happened so fast. Guilt washed upon him. He was supposed to be searching for Dana, not having sex with a stranger.

***

Outside the window, snow descended to the ground. Christmas Eve and Dana was all alone. She missed the lights and spirit of Manhattan. Back home, the wrapped gifts for her friends were all laid on her Christmas tree. Would she have a chance to give them away one day? Sadness crawled inside her. No amount of words could describe what she was going through. Grieving for her father wasn't over. Knowing she may never be alive again was worse. She needed to escape. Clutching her necklace locket, Dana sang the famous, *Silent Night* to keep the holiday spirit going and calm her fears.

She dug into her pocket and removed the three items she had now—a screwdriver, Ginny's Delight's business card, and the driver's watch. Aside from her locket, these were the only precious objects she could think of now aside from her comfortable pajamas and avocado rolls.

Dana had explored every room in the house, but she hadn't paid much attention to the unfinished room. She slipped inside the room and turned on the lights. A cold breeze sent a shiver down her spine. Eying the window, her jaw dropped. Unlike the other windows in the house, this one had no grills. A rush of adrenaline awakened her spirits. *Why didn't I thoroughly check this room before?* She ran back to the living room and bundled up in double pajamas and her jacket.

If she escaped now, who would find her? What if she died of hypothermia before anybody found her? But what options did she have? Dana would rather try and fail then just sit there waiting. She unfastened the screws of the window, and the air gushed in. Heart pounding, she lifted herself up and jumped outside. Tears rolled down her cheeks.

She was free.

Dana marched down the icy pavement. Thank God she wore her gloves and Uggs that day and she was used to the cold weather in Alaska. If anything, her spirit would carry her through. Walking down the catwalk countless times and not having a full meal never bothered her. If she had to walk a hundred miles in this winter cold, she would. *Brrr.*

Chapter 8

At his mother's house in New Jersey, Rob watched his nephews and niece giggle while they watched TV. He visited his family a couple of times a year during Thanksgiving and Christmas. How quickly they grew.

His mother eyed him as she dried the dishes. "When are you going to give me another grandchild?"

He swallowed hard. "I don't know, Mom."

"Oh, c'mon, I know you like that model. She's the only woman you ever brought home to meet me, and she loved my homemade pumpkin pie." She winked.

Bile rose in his throat. He missed Dana more than ever.

"So? Where is she?"

Rob knew he had to tell his mother about Dana's situation so he relayed the story to her.

"What do the police have to say about this?"

Rob checked his iPhone and shook his head. "They think she must have traveled to be alone. Her father just died."

"Maybe they're right."

"No, something's off. She wouldn't just disappear like that." He wished he could open up to his mother, but he couldn't break the confidence Dana entrusted in him.

***

Back at home enjoying her family dinner, Stacy couldn't wipe away her smile. After she told her best friend about Rob, Lisa dared her to be promiscuous. Stacy had to admit it felt good. She never made the first move with a man before, but after her bad break-up with Paul, she wasn't worried about inhibitions anymore. She had fun, and she knew Rob did.

Her mother caught her humming. "Why are you so happy today?"

She stared at her plate, the remnants of lamb chops, some turkey, and a bit of baked potatoes stuck on it. "It's Christmas, Mom. Why shouldn't I be happy?"

Her mother studied her. "Did you see that man again?"

"What man?"

Her father glanced at her. "Is there something you wish to tell us, Stacy?"

"You know who I'm talking about," her mother added.

Folding her arms, Stacy sighed. "Mom, there's nothing wrong with men." Then turning to her father, Stacy added. "If you guys are so miserable then you should have broken up years ago."

Her sister bowed her head down.

Glaring at her, her father said, "I will not allow you to talk to us this way."

Pushing her plate, Stacy rose from her seat. "I'm not hungry." She strode downstairs hoping to get some air. Lights shone from the basement. Her father's workplace.

Stacy shook her head. *It's Christmas and after dinner Dad will do the usual—work!*

She pushed the door and shut her eyes. The flashing lights blinded her.

Opening her eyes, she glanced at the folders scattered on the floor and walked toward the corner where three monitors sat on a desk. *What is he working on?*

As she leaned on the desk, the monitors lit up. "Oh no." She covered her face to block out the photos of young, naked teenagers having sex with older men and women. "No, this can't be real."

A wave of anxiety washed over her. She picked up the folders from the floor—files of different teenage women, all nude. Unable to stomach this, she rushed toward the exit and bumped into her father who stared at her with cold, grim, guarded eyes.

"What are you doing here?"

She gasped, but no words came from her mouth. Shoving him away, Stacy dashed to the streets and didn't look back. A cold shiver ran through her spine. How could he do this? How long had he been doing this pornography business? She had always thought the restaurant was their only business and he spent hours in the basement balancing their sales reports and expenses. Did her mother know about this? If she did, how could her mother keep this from her? A knot formed in her stomach. This made her sick.

Still rushing, Stacy tried not to focus on the cold, or that no one else was around. Without her thick coat, she wouldn't last long out here.

I'm not going back there. I'll stay in a hotel if I have to. She needed to call her sister. Racing thoughts occupied her as she hurried, having no time to pause to catch her breath. Moments later, she heard strong footsteps following her along with a dark shadow. Fear crawled inside her, and all she could do was run faster.

***

Rob's iPhone vibrated, and he bolted right up from his bed. Glancing at the clock, he moaned. Five a.m., who could be calling me this early. "This is Rob."

"Rob Hanson, this is Detective Schultz. Officer Jones gave me your number. I'm so—"

"I expected you to call me last night. I thought you'd forgotten about me. Do you have any leads about the case?"

"I'm afraid we found an unidentified body." He paused. "She matches your description. I need you to come and meet me at the morgue."

Rob's heart sank like a deflated balloon. *It can't be Dana.* "I'll be there. Please give me the address."

***

"Please to meet you," Rob greeted Detective Schultz, a middle-aged man with a receding hairline and pronounced beer belly, who seemed more relaxed compared to the more serious Officer Jones.

"Thank you for coming in right away," Detective Schultz shook Rob's hand before signaling the examiner to lower the sheets.

The mixture of rubbing alcohol and blood made Rob dizzy. He flexed his hands back and forth wanting to escape the enclosed morgue.

Rob's throat constricted as the body was displayed.

"Slashed throat and multiple beatings," The examiner relayed to both of them.

"Oh, my God." Covering his face, Rob vomited everything he ate earlier that evening on the floor.

Detective Schultz patted him on the back and gave him a towel. "Is this the woman you are talking about?"

Catching his breath and unable to look at the body again, Rob shook his head. "That's not Dana. Thank God." He stuttered.

The detective glanced at the examiner and gestured to leave them alone. The examiner nodded. "You'll need to come with me to the station."

"Oh, God. Who would possibly do this?"

***

At the station, Rob sat across from the detective's office while he recorded their conversation. "State your name and your relationship to Dana Simmons."

"I already told you in the car. I gave all the info to Officer Jones."

"We need this for standard procedures."

Rob followed his orders.

"And prior to Dana's disappearance, you never saw her?"

"I only saw her before she left for Alaska."

"And what where you doing at Ginny's cafe for the past two days?"

"You've been following me?" Rob leaned back.

The detective gestured for Rob to continue.

"Well, like I told Officer Jones, somebody left a fruitcake for Dana." He crossed his legs. "Wait a minute, are you trying to interrogate me? Shouldn't you be investigating where Dana is?"

"Don't you worry, I have my team taking care of all that." He folded his arms, and the smile on his face disappeared. "What time were you at Ginny's?"

Rob glanced at the ceiling. "After three o'clock."

The detective shrugged. "Just standard questions. The woman who served you, Stacy Kestav, did you see her after that?"

His rendezvous with Stacy remained fresh on his mind—her luscious lips, vibrant personality... Something inside him wanted to see her again. "Why are you asking me about Stacy? I thought we were here to discuss about Dana. Is there anything wrong with Stacy?"

Detective Schultz's eyes were guarded.

"Detective, I wish you would cut to the chase." Lips puckered, he added, "Like I said, I went to Ginny's because the day my friend, Dana disappeared, she received a fruitcake from an anonymous person who bought it from Ginny's. Take a look at this card." He handed it to the detective. "I was there to find clues."

Detective Shultz read the card then leaned closer. "Stacy was reported missing by her parents a few hours ago. It hasn't been forty-eight hours yet. We suspect her disappearance has something to do with Dana."

"What?"

Detective Schultz straightened his shoulders and looked at him straight in the eye. "It seems that these two women have one thing in common." He pointed at Rob. "You."

Clenching his fists, Rob blurted out. "This isn't how it seems. When I was at the café, Stacy and I engaged in a conversation." Tilting his head, he said, "Her mother didn't like her chatting with the customers as she had to work." Wanting to provide full disclosure, Rob added. "She passed by my place to apologize then wanted to have her pictures taken."

"Pictures?"

"I'm a photographer."

"Right."

"One thing led to another, then the next thing you know, we had sex."

"After you had sex, where did you go?"

"I stayed home and went to sleep after Stacy left."

"Can somebody confirm that?"

"This is bull shit! I told you, Stacy came to my house." Rob tightened his jaw.

Shaking his head, the detective said, "You expect me to believe your story that this woman came to your house to have sex." Detective Schultz coughed. "And now she vanished, just like your girlfriend." He leaned back. "You don't have an alibi to prove your whereabouts Mr. Hanson."

"I know what you're trying to imply, Detective, that I have something to do with this, but you're wasting your time, thinking that way instead of looking for Dana. You guys are slackers."

***

Marcy Simmons banged the wall from her room. How could they leave her confined in a room with no windows and just a mirror? If only she hadn't gone to her husband's memorial service. None of this would have happened. But she just had to get a glimpse of her daughter Dana once again to see what a fine, beautiful woman she became. As a result, here she was, back where she started.

The door flung open, and a short man with a pot belly and greasy face popped in with a tray of lunch.

She immediately shut her eyes and pretended to sleep.

He slapped her face. "Wake up, sleepyhead."

Massaging her cheek, Marcy sat up. "You seem to be amused by hurting people. Did your parents abuse you as a child?"

He slapped her again.

Swaying her head side to side, she added, "That confirms it."

"Look, lady." He pointed his finger too close to her eye. "If it were up to me, I would have killed you right away."

"Oh, you poor thing, can't make your own decisions."

Eyes open wide, he planted his hands on her neck and began to choke her.

Gasping for air, Marcy poked her nails into his eyeballs.

He released her and covered his eyes. "You bitch! I swear, I will kill you next time." He slammed the door and turned the lock.

Marcy examined her neck in the mirror. Red marks marred her skin. *I will be the one to kill them.*

***

Stacy Kestav awoke, her head throbbing. *Where am I?* Darkness enveloped her, but still she could spot steel bars. "Help, somebody help me."

"They can't hear you," a young female voice laced with a hushed accent.

Blinking her eyes, she caught a glimpse of a teenage girl with a square jaw and prominent features who seemed younger than Stacy outside her cell. "Where are we?"

"We're underground. There are a lot of us down here," the girl said. "We were brought here from Russia."

Stacy's heart sank like a flat tire. *How can I escape?* "What's your name and how long have you been here?"

"Weeks. I'm Valentina. They took my twin sister and I away from my family," she said. "They promised my parents they would give us a better life in America, but instead we are told to do dirty things with men, lots of men, in front of a camera."

A sound of voices echo.

"Sh, they're coming."

Stacy closed her eyes in dread.

Chapter 9

Dana felt she had been running for eternity. There was no sight of civilization as the end of the pavement only led to a dirt road. A glance at her watch revealed it had been almost two hours, and she wasn't sure she if she'd been going the right direction.

She gazed at the sky above. "Please help me, Lord."

Shortly, a ray of light appeared in front of her. She waved her arms in the air as hope rejuvenated her.

A black BMW slowed down and stopped in front of her. Dana smiled and approached the passenger door.

The door flung open, and a man stepped out. "Are you lost?"

Dana's smile vanished. Skully. This time, he was not alone. A woman stepped out of the car and faced her.

Frozen, Dana stared at the lady, the one person she recognized and could never forget, the woman who left her when she was ten years old. She had shattered her life and killed her father emotionally.

Adrenaline rose inside, her but she kept her compose by pretending she didn't know her.

Skully approached Dana and pushed her toward her mother. "I told you I know where your mother is, and now she's right in front of you."

Her mother put on a straight face and didn't once flinch. "That's my daughter? I don't think so."

Her words dug into Dana's heart, but she knew her mother faked her reaction and remained calm.

"You heard what she said. I'm not her daughter, so will you just let us all go? You're wasting your time when you should be looking for the right person," Dana said.

Skully banged Dana's head onto the car.

***

Dana opened her eyes feeling a fierce throbbing pain behind her head. Two people were sitting beside her, but she couldn't see them clearly. "Where am I?"

A woman's voice spoke. "You need to rest."

Flashes of memories—the dirt road, Skully, her mother—assaulted Dana. She bolted upright. "You did this to me."

"Sh!" Her mother rubbed Dana's shoulders. "I never thought I'd ever see you again."

Although her angelic face tempted to soften Dana's emotions, she blurted, "How could you leave us?"

Dana had rehearsed over and over again what she would have done had she seen her mother. She always believed her mother was out there somewhere, never had found closure.

Her mother paced around the room. Although she'd aged, her skin was still flawless, her body trim. "If I told you the reason I left, you would understand."

A roller coaster of emotions grilled upon Dana as she fought back tears. "I was ten."

"I followed all your shows," she said in a hushed tone. "Cut every clipping and stored photos of you. I couldn't believe how my daughter blossomed into a beautiful woman. I'm so proud of you."

Dana affixed her stare at the windowpane. "How about I tell you how you ripped my childhood apart and only after Dad died did I discover my whole life has been a lie."

Marcy drew in a breath. "Your father was a good man. He took care of you. "

"Really, Mom? Because he died the day you vanished."

"I never stopped loving you both. You have to believe me."

Taking deep breaths, Dana faced her mother and couldn't say a word. Her head continued to throb from the bang.

"Remember how I used to braid your hair? You always wanted to apply lipstick like me."

Dana glared. "There's no use bringing back the memories. They're all tainted with lies."

Marcy gave her a blank stare. "Your life is in danger, Dana. That's why I left. So I could protect you."

"Tell me about it. Each day I spend with you leads me closer to my death. Actually, I think I'm already in hell."

Marcy sighed. "I don't where to begin."

The sound of footsteps came close.

Dana didn't budge, one hand exposed while the other clutched the screwdriver tight, ready to pounce at Skully if he attacked her again.

Marcy eyed the door. "He's coming."

***

A shiny, squeaky pair of shoes approached Rob as he sat at the waiting room of Atty. Chan's office. A tall Asian man in his twenties, dressed in a fine, pale gray Armani suit. "Rob Hanson, I'm Stanley Chan. Pleasure to meet you."

They shook hands.

"Nice to meet you. You were able to get a hold of my father?"

"Yeah, I assume you know he's in Costa Rica —"

"Right." Rob leaned one foot to the wall. His father was busy with his new wife trotting the globe. He scrutinized the lawyer from head to toe. "And how many cases have you handled?"

Straightening his shoulders, Stanley grinned. "Don't be fooled by my looks. Your father works with the best lawyers." He led Rob inside his office. "Let's discuss more inside."

Stanley circled around his desk and plopped himself on the chair.

Rob sat across him, glancing at color-coded folders, noticing how his desk was polished like his shoes.

Stanley smirked. "I know, I know. I suffer from OCD, but take my condition to your advantage since I will ensure I produce quality work with the investigation."

"I trust my father, and I know you won't let me down."

"Thank you. Anyway, here's what I gathered." He handed folders to Rob. "There have been five reported missing women in Manhattan during the past year. Dana is the fifth one and Stacy the sixth."

Rob breezed through the documents. "How do we know they're related to Dana's case?"

"The women are all between twenty-eight and twenty-nine years old except for Stacy."

Rob paused. "Wait a minute. Dana just turned thirty."

"Is that so?"

"Yes, December fifteen."

"Hmm." Stanley grabbed his red pen and marked his notes.

"And what does this have to do with Stacy? I assume she's much younger than these women."

Stanley leaned forward. "That's what I need to investigate. The judge granted a search warrant, and they didn't find anything suspicious at her parent's house. They're simple Russian immigrants who speak very little English."

Rob stomped his feet. "They're hiding something. I can feel it. Did you check the café?"

"Rob, I have to warn you to be careful. You can't assume anything based on feelings. Right now, the media is pinning you down and you have to maintain a low profile."

"I can't believe this."

"I hate to say this, but I believe it would be best that you don't stay at your loft. I can set you up at a motel in Brooklyn."

"What about my projects?"

"It will only be temporary. And don't do anything stupid."

***

FBI Agents Felicia and Kerry sat on the benches across Central park, each chewing a hot dog. Kerry watched tourists, joggers and executives passing through the park.

"Something tells me this kidnapping is personal. Six attractive blonds. What do you make out of that?" Felicia asked.

"One Puerto Rican." He wiped mustard from his lips. "Tell me what your theory is."

"The person doesn't seem like he picked this women at random. The perpetrator must have studied every move, their routines, where they go. I think the Puerto Rican lady was to divert our attention from the criminal's patterns. My hunch tells me that this criminal doesn't work alone."

"Possible."

"The only thing that puzzles me is that Dana Simmons turned thirty recently. Why didn't her captor take her before then?"

Kerry faced her. "You have a point there. Detective Schultz informed me that her friend Rob said her father just died."

"Ah." Felicia gave a sharp jerk of a nod. "Do you think that guy Rob has anything to do with this?"

Kerry pursed his lips. "I don't know. He knew both Dana and Stacy."

She threw a pebble on the ground. "I believe Rob has nothing to do with their case. He came to the police to find his friend, and when they shrugged him off, he sought answers for himself, which led to Stacy's disappearance."

"But that could be his cover up."

"He might have a list of women who have modeled for him and that should give us clues in case this person targets another woman again."

"Felicia, tell me again why I need you?"

She poked him. "Wake up. We've got work to do."

Chapter 10

Muffled cries filtered from the other room. Dana failed to open the locked door. The weeping grew deafening. She leaned her ears against the wall and heard Skully, her mother, and two, no three, no four women screaming. *What is happening out there?*

"If you guys don't shut the fuck up," Skully yelled, "I will sink your head inside the toilet and leave you there."

Silence descended, and Dana dashed back to her bed in case Skully came. Questions plagued her. Why was she here? Who were these women, and what would happen next?

"You need to let me know once and for all who is your daughter, Marcy!"

Dana jerked back at the raw anger in Skully's voice.

"I told you I don't have any daughter."

Dana covered her face. They were after her now. Guilt washed upon her. Her father was right. Her mother only wished to protect her.

But from what exactly?

***

Rob sneezed for the sixth time that evening. He cleaned the mold from his bathroom and stared at the cracked linoleum tiles. Being a photographer taught him how to appreciate beauty and art, but there wasn't anything attractive about this dingy motel.

Rob wiped the tears from his face as he clutched the phone. "I'm sorry, Mom. I never wished to disappoint you this way."

"My son, I know you have nothing to do with these women. I don't wish to turn on the TV anymore because the news just devastates me."

"Don't believe them. The media will do anything to destroy me. That's how they make a living. In the meantime, be strong and pray for me."

"I will. You take care of yourself."

"I love you, Mom."

***

Kerry and Felicia studied Ginny's Delights from the corner table inside. Closing time approached, and both Mr. and Mrs. Kestav were cleaning the counters. No more patrons lingered in the café.

Kerry nudged his partner on the side. "We've been here three times. Nothing has changed."

"Sh. You're too complacent," Felicia whispered. She raised her chin. "Just look at them, especially Mrs. Kestav. She's nervous as hell. Trust me. I know they're hiding something."

Mr. Kestav approached them, his hair gelled to one side, both hands inside his pocket. "Agents, any updates with the case?"

Kerry stared at him. "You tell us, Mr. Kestav. Who would want to kidnap your daughter? Your sweet daughter who had a whole life ahead of her. Wasn't she supposed to leave for Paris?"

"Yes," he choked out in between tears. You have to find the bastard who took her."

Mrs. Kestav squeezed herself between them with a tray of desserts and two waters. "Please enjoy these goodies."

The couple sat beside the agents.

"So…" Felicia licked the chocolate icing of the decadent cake. "What's Stacy's favorite dessert?"

Mr. and Mrs. Kestav exchanged glances.

Mr. Kestav cleared his throat. "Stacy was actually a diabetic, and most of our desserts are made from real sugar."

"She was the one who created the special sugar-free desserts," Mrs. Kestav added.

After taking a sip of his water, Kerry said, "Must be difficult for a diabetic to be surrounded by sugar. Is this the reason why she wanted to leave?"

Stacy's sister stepped forward from the back. "Mom, everything's done. Can I walk ahead?"

"Natasha, we won't be long," Mrs. Kestav said. "I don't want you walking alone out there."

Natasha rolled her eyes. "I'll wait here then."

Kerry rose from his seat with his plate. "I'll take this to the counter." He followed Natasha to the back kitchen where she sat glued to her iPhone. "Must be lonely without your sister."

The skinny blond teenager didn't budge as she continued to text. "For once, I don't want to keep talking about her."

"My little brother died when I was twelve." He sat beside her.

She glanced at him. "How?"

"Asthma attack. All the attention was focused on his death. I not only felt left out, but I felt like I didn't exist."

Natasha pushed her phone aside. "That's exactly how I feel. When my parents talk, it's always about what Stacy would have wanted. And when they're not talking, I can taste their tears in our desserts."

"You can't erase her disappearance, but you can help us find clues."

She nodded. "You're right. I do miss her so much."

"And you're allowed to miss her." He handed her his business card. "If you find anything suspicious, please give me a call."

"Thanks." She tucked the card inside her pocket.

**

Five minutes later, the agents climbed into the car. Felicia blasted the music, but Kerry turned down the volume.

"C'mon. You're never too old for rock music." Felicia brushed back her loose hair.

His radio beeped. "Agent Wayne, we received an anonymous tip that four blond women were sighted being shoved inside a car by a man with a sleeveless shirt and tattoo stopped at a 7-11 in New Jersey," Officer Jones said.

"Copy that. Do they have the exact location?"

"Sending you guys the address now. Witness said the women looked filthy and gaunt."

"Thank you." He glanced at Felicia. "Maybe you can start blasting the radio as we take a drive to New Jersey."

Felicia checked her iPhone. "Hmmm, I know exactly where that is. My hometown."

"You never told me you grew up in New Jersey."

Bobbing her head from side to side, Felicia said, "Jersey Shore."

***

Dana waited. When her door opened and her mother entered, Dana pounced on her like a prey. She shoved her mother to the door and pushed the screwdriver at her throat.

Beads of sweat poured from Marcy's forehead.

"Sh," she whispered. "I'm not going to let them hurt us." She cleared her throat and yelled, "You better tell me everything, or I will kill you. I don't care what happens to me."

Skully popped inside. "Now, here comes the feisty woman. She surely takes after you, Marcy."

Marcy eyed the screwdriver and elbowed Dana in her stomach, knocking her down to the floor. "I make the rules around here." Turning to Skully, Marcy added, "For the tenth time, I have no daughter."

Dana lifted onto all fours and kicked Skully in the crotch .

"You bitch!" Skully doubled over.

Dana said to the four women sitting huddled together in the living room. "C'mon. Let's go."

The four women, resigned and filthy, shook their heads.

One petite blond lady with a ponytail said, "We can't go anywhere. They will find us."

Dana pulled them up. "We can't give up. We're five. Please."

They followed her to the door. Dana's heart leaped as the door wasn't locked. She dashed outside with the four women trailing behind and inhaled the fresh air.

From the corner of her eye, Dana spotted her mother running after her, but Skully pulled her back. Dana halted, but her mother signaled her to leave. Her heart sank. *I will see her again.*

"Do you know where we are?" Dana asked.

The curly-haired blond inched her way beside Dana. "I overheard the man say we're near Jersey Shore."

"Hmm." Dana raced to the left. "You guys have to follow me. I tried that route." She pointed to the right. "It didn't lead me anywhere. I'm assuming if we go south, we should reach the ocean."

An hour later, the five women still followed the dirt road, catching their breath.

"We can't stop," Dana warned.

The Puerto Rican spoke up. "We need to know why they took us? I'm Maria, and this is Belinda, Jane, and Rosie. What's your story?

The women exchanged information sharing a common way of being abducted.

"The lady in the house is my mother," Dana said.

They gasped as Dana narrated how Marcy disappeared when she was ten and finished with her father's letter.

"Did your mother tell you why?" Belinda asked.

"All she said is that I was in danger."

"That's what she told all of us," Jane said. "We were all in an abandoned house before they transferred us to where you were. They all asked us if she was our mother."

"I was the first one," Rosie added.

"Did they rape you guys? What did they tell you?" Dana asked.

They shook their head.

"No, they would come bring food and psychologically play with your mind and then disappear and come after two days," Maria said.

"They did the same thing with me."

"Wait a minute," Rosie said. "You're a supermodel, right? I've seen your face in magazines."

Dana nodded. "Yeah, but I just turned thirty and nobody's going to want me."

"You're still beautiful. I'm twenty-nine and I would love to look like you," Rosie said.

"Me too. I'm twenty-eight," Maria added.

"Twenty-eight, "Jane said.

"Twenty-nine," Belinda chimed in.

"Hmm, looks like our captors are trying to figure out who is her daughter. I mean look at all of us. We're almost the same height and built," Dana said.

The ladies exchanged glances.

"We better start walking." Dana glanced at her watch. "We don't want to be out here at nighttime and die of hypothermia.

"I'm feeling so cold," Rosie said.

"Rosie, the hike will do you good," Belinda said.

Dana went ahead. She had to believe she would reach Jersey Shore soon.

Chapter 11

Rob entered Ginny's Delights.

Mrs. Kestav froze. "We're closed. Didn't you see the sign? Please leave."

"Please, Mrs. Kestav, I'm sorry about what happened to your daughter, but you have to believe I had nothing to do with her disappearance."

Mrs. Kestav picked up the phone. "I'm going to call the police if you don't leave."

"Wait." He raised his hands up. "I'm telling you the truth. I have a friend named Dana who is missing, and I believe it has to be connected to your daughter."

Mrs. Kestav mumbled something in Russian.

Rob took a deep breath. It did nothing to help calm him. Nothing would, not until he saw Dana again, alive and safe, preferably in his arms. The clock kept ticking. Every minute she was gone could mean she could be gone forever. "The day Dana disappeared, she received a fruitcake from Ginny's Delights. That's why I came here that first day."

Mrs. Kestav studied him. "Do you know how many customers we have?"

"I know."

"Because of you, my daughter is gone. Get out before I call the cops. You're the last person I want to see here."

***

Fifteen minutes had passed since the women escaped.

"Hurry up, guys," Dana said, looking behind her. "We don't have all day."

"My asthma is acting up." Rosie threaded through the snow, her wheezing audible.

Maria was able to sneak out bottled water and she handed it to Rosie. "This should help."

A wave of snow flushed through them like lightning.

Losing her balance, Dana stumbled and spotted an SUV Runner in front of her. "Shit." She clung to Belinda and Jane. "We need to get out of here."

The SUV swerved. The door flung open, and out stepped Skully. In two massive steps, he grabbed Dana's hair. "You think you can escape." He grabbed his M-16 and shot at Belinda, Jane, Maria, and Rosie.

They all collapsed, blood oozing from their chest.

"No," Dana yelled, her body shaking. "How could you do this? They're innocent victim and don't deserve this.

Skully gripped her arm so tightly she grit her teeth to prevent crying out. He shoved her inside the SUV. "That's what you get for trying to flee."

"Please don't hurt me." She pushed him but he didn't budge.

"It's your lucky day."

A Honda Pilot pulled over to the side, and the redheaded driver popped his head out from the window.

"Dump these bodies and get the hell out of here," Skully instructed before slamming the door.

The horror on the women's faces haunted Dana as she closed her eyes. Tears trickled down her cheeks as she silently sobbed.

The ride was eerily silent. It was now New Year's Eve. She had survived another day.

Her mother greeted them as they stepped inside the house. "Where are the other ladies?"

Skully didn't say a word.

Dana wanted to fling her arms around her mother. Of course she refrained. Hands trembling, she removed her Uggs. "I need to take a shower."

"No more tricks," Skully warned. "I'll be in the bedroom. You need to leave the door open."

Dana glanced at her mother.

On cue, Marcy watched Skully. "I don't think the bathroom has any towels."

Skully growled and left the room.

Her mother whispered. "Honey, I'm sorry—"

"I know you did the right thing. *I'm* sorry for being so mean and hostile to you, but we can't chat about this now. We need to escape before he kills us both. Follow me."

Dana removed the screwdriver from inside her pocket and clutched it. *Now or never.* She darted outside the room where Skully was on the phone speaking in a hushed tone, his back towards Dana. Dana dashed toward Skully and aimed the screwdriver directly for his eye. Skully elbowed her face. Dana ducked and ended up plunging the screwdriver into his arm.

"You bitch!"

Her mother screamed when Skully grabbed her leg.

Dana ran fast as she could out of the front door, oblivious to the cold creeping inside her body. She looked behind, hoping her mom was able to catch up with her, but disappointment washed upon her. Tears pooled her vision when air escaped her lungs. She could hear her mother's screams, and Skully yelling after her.

Dana prayed hard, wishing somebody would rescue her so she could come back for her mother. No sooner did she finish her prayer when she heard a deafening sound of a propeller. Bright lights shone from above as a helicopter made a sharp curve and landed in front of her.

A tall man in a suit stepped out and approached her. "Dana Simmons." A wave of anxiety crashed upon her when he gripped her arm. "You're coming with me."

"No," she screamed, pushing him away."Don't take me back there."

"I'm here to help you." The man reached into his pocket.

"I don't believe you." She pushed him.

The man pulled her inside.

"Please!" Dana yanked her arm away, but it was too late. She had a new captor now.

***

After a trip to the Jersey shore to get some leads, Kerry and Felicia drove back to New York to inspect Dana's apartment. Kerry looked underneath the bed.

Felicia studied her closet. "I wish I had half the pairs of shoes and purses she has."

"What is it with you women with shoes and purses? I can't seem to figure you ladies out."

"That's one thing a man will never understand." Felicia peered into a drawer and found Dana's lingerie. "My, my, this woman just loves the colors black and white."

"Must be easier to match to clothes, I guess." Kerry shrugged. What did he know about it?

"Believe me, I prefer pastel shades over black and white."

He chuckled. "You're a girly girl."

"Yup." She checked out the shoes. "This woman was abducted. A beautiful and glamorous model like Dana Simmons is not going to leave her home without her clothes. I perceive her to be the type of lady who travels with two suitcases for a weekend trip with her matching entourage. And surely, somebody ought to recognize that woman."

"You're right. Let's hope she's not dead." He rubbed his scruffy chin. "But we've searched everything from Rob's apartment. Her last call was to him. You've also gone over the tapes."

"Yeah, but we still have the mysterious fruitcake gift and card that doesn't make sense."

Felicia followed him to the kitchen and found bread crumbs on the counter and two books. She picked up the books and found a folded note then glanced at Kerry and read the note aloud.

They exchanged glances.

Kerry's cell phone rang. "Agent Wayne here," he paused. "Yep. We'll be there."

She raised his eyebrows.

"They found four women dead near Jersey shore."

"God bless their souls. We gotta go back there."

"Wait." Kerry picked up another call. "Yes, U.S. Marshall Collins. What can I do for you?" He eyed Felicia. "Uh-huh, you found her."

Chapter 12

Dana rubbed her eyes and rose from a leather couch. *Where am I?* She sat inside an office with a desk and an American flag behind it. She spotted three men were whispering, but she couldn't overhear them. A woman had her eyes glued to a folder and another man sat in the corner with a sketchpad.

A man with hair gelled to the side turned around and nodded. "You're awake."

Swallowing hard, she stood from the couch and almost stumbled.

He clasped her arm. She spied a mole on his cheek. This man had been the one to pull her inside the helicopter before she passed out.

"Don't be afraid, you're safe now. Coffee?" he asked.

"Where am I?"

The tallest man joined them. "Dana Simmons, why don't we get you some breakfast? You must be starving."

"I'm not eating until you tell me where I am. You can't manipulate me into doing what you want." She raised her voice.

A man dropped the file on the coffee table and approached her. "I'm FBI special Agent Kerry Wayne and this is my partner Agent Felicia Raymond. We are so sorry for what happened, and we're so glad our team rescued you today."

With her hands planted on her hips, Dana mumbled, "Can somebody please explain what's going on?"

The men exchanged glances.

The tallest man unbuttoned his suit and sat down on the couch. "Very well, let me introduce ourselves." He rubbed his chin. "I'm U.S. Marshall Collins, and this is U.S. Marshall Adams. This is Roger, the sketch artist."

Dana didn't blink.

"Please sit down for what we are going to tell you today will change your life," U.S. Marshall Collins added.

Agents Raymond and Wayne moved to the corner and stood there.

Dana sat down, tucking a strand of hair behind her ears.

"Ms. Simmons," U.S. Marshall Collins began. "Your life is in danger."

She gave a hysterical laugh. "Tell me about it. I'm surprised I'm still alive."

U.S. Marshall Adams cleared his throat. "It's more than you think."

"My mother's still out there."

U.S. Marshall Collins leaned closer. His coffee breath worsened her splitting headache. "We tried our very best to check the surroundings but couldn't find a trace of your mother. You need to tell us about the men who captured you."

"The shorter guy had a raspy voice and a dagger with a skull tattoo on his right arm. The redheaded driver never talked much. And those women, they killed all of them." She coughed, wanting to puke.

They jotted down the details.

"Roger can work with you about the details of his features," U.S. Marshall Adams said.

"Your mother was part of the WITSEC program," U.S. Marshall Collins divulged.

"What?" Dana straightened her shoulders. "Do you mean the Witness Protection Program?"

"That's correct. Your mother was a prime witness of a crime before you were born. She was a Broadway actress in the Big Apple until she discovered that her Russian manager was part of the mob whose business involved the sex trafficking of minors. Your mother witnessed first-hand a container filled with young Russian women who were turned into prostitutes. She also saw them kill women who tried to escape."

Dana rubbed her head. This was too much for her to process. Her gaze sought out the door. *I wish I could escape it all. This is just a dream... No. A nightmare I can wake up from.*

But U.S. Marshall Collins continued to rattle on. "We plucked her out from her glamorous life in Manhattan."

Dana nodded for him to continue. How had her mother felt when she had to move? Like her mother, Dana loved Manhattan.

"And we let her live a new life in Alaska." His eyes suddenly guarded, he averted his gaze.

"Tell me."

"Your father isn't actually your father.

Dana kicked the chair.

"We had to take her far away as possible where nobody would find her—"

"How dare you tell me all these lies. My father was a good father. He's the only father I'll ever have and just because he's dead, you have no right to tell me this."

U.S. Marshall Collins continued. "We're aware this may be a lot of information for you, but we're here to help."

Dana took deep breaths then covered her face. "I don't believe you. If he's not my father, then who is?"

The U.S. Marshalls exchanged glances.

"Ugh, don't tell me it's her manager. The Russian guy?"

U.S. Marshall Collins stared at the carpet.

Dana demanded. "You said I need to know everything."

He nodded.

"This is insane."

Agent Raymond said, "Your father protected her and raised you as his own. He knew that at any time, she would have to leave given the circumstances. From what we've gathered, it was your father who pleaded for you to stay with him. He couldn't bear losing you."

Dana welled up in tears. "And my mother? Did she love him?"

U.S. Marshall Collins added, "She told us that she learned to love him. Your mother never wanted to leave you, but when news reached the Russian mafia that she was in Alaska, she only had one choice—to escape. They weren't aware she had a daughter until…"

Dana sighed, rubbing her arms. Why couldn't they be a normal family? Why couldn't she have had two parents who took her to school or had barbecues during the rare sunny days in their backyard like her classmates did? Now she discovered that her father whom she loved dearly was not her father. Now she knew why she was hardly allowed to go out and why her father built that tree house for her. The tree house wasn't her only sanctuary, but a place where her father could look out for her. "Until?"

"You're a splitting image of your mother, Dana. You're in every magazine and commercial. Somebody must have put two and two together," U.S. Marshall Collins said. "We suspect your father tried to reach your mother before he died."

Dana covered her face. "Those men who kidnapped me, who are they? They've also taken my mother and they killed those other women."

U.S. Marshall Collins asked. "Can you tell us what happened when you came back to New York after your father's death?"

"I was mourning and didn't want to go out. I declined invitations to holiday parties and modeling projects. I couldn't bring myself to move on."

"Did anything suspicious occur?" U.S. Marshall Adams asked.

"Well, aside from my lawyer giving me my father's letter, I did receive a fruitcake from Ginny's Delights. I left the fruitcake and took a walk in Central Park. That's where they kidnapped me."

"Ginny's Delights?" U.S. Marshall Collins frowned.

"Yes. And I found their business card inside the drawer in that house, the one I was kept in."

"Ginny's Delights is right down the street. We usually have coffee or desserts. That means this man has been following us," Agent Wayne said.

"You guys are not clear. First you tell me that it's a Russian mob, and now you tell me it's a man. What's the real story here?"

U.S. Marshall Collins cleared his throat. "Your biological father, Anton Marcovic, passed away a year ago. He had been searching for your mother and never found her. We learned from an anonymous tip that before he passed away, he discovered he had a daughter and had been hoping to track you down until his heart gave way."

"Great. In one day, I find out that my mother is part of the WITSEC, my father is not my real father, and my biological father is part of the Russian mob and is now dead. Isn't that enough?" Her tummy growled, but she couldn't imagine eating after what she'd been through. Her life would never be normal again. "If he's already dead, why are they still after my mother?"

"He has a son."

"A son?" She paused. "I have a half brother?"

"Vladimir."

She swallowed hard trying to process all the information. "My half brother."

"Technically, he's not. Your father adopted Vladimir when he was five." U.S. Marshall Collins said. "You don't have to be afraid. We are here to help you."

Dana shook her head. "You're not here to protect me. You're going to strip my life like you did with my mother. Do you know what you did to her? To me? Do you know how hard it is for me to be close to people fearing that I can lose them? I've never had a long relationship." She broke down crying. "I travel a lot, I keep a bright smile on my face, but nobody knows the emptiness I feel inside."

"I'm sorry," U.S. Marshall Adams said.

"Tell me, U.S. Marshall Adams, did you grow up with a mother? Did you have somebody kiss you goodbye before you went to school?"

U.S. Marshall Adams looked away.

"You're never going to give me back the years I lost with my mother. You destroyed my life, and nobody, not even my father, had the decency to tell me the truth. How dare you!"

"We're very sorry, Dana," Agent Raymond said.

She glared at them. "So this is it? You're going to control me like you did with my mother?" You said you would protect her, but after all these years, they've found her."

"We did the best we could."

"Really? Up 'till now, you haven't been able to bust the Russian mob." She stomped her foot. "Why is that, U.S. Marshall Collins? And what makes you so sure that you can protect me?"

Chapter 13

Moments later, despite desperate pleading from Dana, the U.S. Marshals didn't say a word as she chewed her tofu in the same office. What lay in store for her? She lifted her chin and stared at them. "Why are you keeping me as a prisoner?"

U.S. Marshall Collins spoke softly. "We are here to protect you."

"You keep saying that." Tears prickled her eyes. How she wished she'd hugged and kissed her mother. Bile rose in her throat. It would be a miracle if she saw her mother again. She hated her biological father, and now her step-brother was trying to finish the job. He would not just kill her mother. He would kill her as well.

Agent Wayne sat across from Dana while Agent Raymond leaned against the wall.

"We have a few questions to ask you about your friend, Rob Hanson," Agent Wayne said.

"Rob? Is he in trouble?"

Agent Wayne exchanged glances with Agent Raymond before facing Dana. "A Russian young lady named Stacy Kestav is missing."

"We don't have any reason to believe Rob's responsible for Stacy's disappearance, but he is now involved since he came searching for you" Agent Raymond added, handing Dana a business card.

Dana's heart sank when she read Ginny's Delights.

"Rob went to your apartment, and they told him about the fruitcake."

"And the good friend that Rob is, he went to Ginny's Delights to get some answers," Dana finished.

Circling the table, Agent Raymond nodded. "Stacy visited his studio and he took photos of her."

Dana shrugged. "Rob's harmless. He's a photographer and agent."

"Nude photos." Agent Wayne lifted his eyebrows. "I don't know how well you know your friend, but he admitted to having sex with Ms. Kestav."

"I don't believe you." Since when did Rob have casual sex?

"He hasn't stopped looking for you," Agent Wayne said.

Tears spilled down Dana's cheeks. "Can't you tell him I'm alive? He's my best friend. Is that too much to ask?"

Agent Raymond's eyes swept the carpet.

"Please," she begged.

But the U.S. Marshalls escorted Agents Wayne and Raymond to the door and murmured, "Thanks again for rescuing Dana. We will take care of her from now on."

"I know you need something from me." She glared at both U.S. Marshalls. "Unlike my mother, you're not going to manipulate me. We will do this my way."

U.S. Marshall Collins grabbed a stack of folders from his desk and returned to the couch. He opened each file. "This is Natalia Akulov. She was thirteen when she was taken away from her family in Russia and smuggled to America." He opened another folder. "This is Valeria Bogdanov and her twin sister Valentina, both fifteen, and this—"

"I've seen enough."

"Anton was their leader, but there are others involved in this filthy business and we're trying to track them down. We know they have an underground headquarters in Manhattan and we're this close to busting them, but we have to plan this well."

"Why can't you just kill them all?" she countered.

"We're talking about a mob here. They come in packs, and until we track everyone involved, there's no guarantee they will stop," Agent Adams said.

"What's in it for me? Will I get my life back? Will I get everything that I lost?"

U.S. Marshall Collins pursed his lips. "We are here to protect you."

"You keep saying that."

U.S. Marshall Collins handed Dana a scrapbook.

"What's this?" She flipped through the pages where she saw photos of her modeling career. As she reached the end of the page, she saw nine words written in bold with a red sharpie: Why didn't you tell me we had a daughter?

Dana tossed the scrapbook on the floor.

"After your mother left, she was on the run. The Marcovic clan always came close. She must have lived in forty cities before the mob found this scrapbook."

Pain shattered like a broken glass in the inside.

"Now that you know the truth, Dana, we're requesting that you cooperate with us."

Dana didn't budge. This wasn't a request. More like a command. Dana would just be like her mother, living in fear and looking over her shoulder if someone was chasing her. She knew how this would all end—always be alone, surrounded by strangers, living a fake life, never getting close to anyone.

What difference did it make? Her life was over.

U.S. Marshall Collins unbuttoned his suit and sat across Dana. "I know this is a huge change for you."

Dana glared at him. "Quit the small talk and let's get down to business. Just tell me what the next step is."

"Very well." He folded his arms.

Dana faced him, gritting her teeth. "And if I'm in this game, I need all the info I can get about this Vladimir—his job, what he likes, where he lives, and what keeps him awake at night."

He crossed his legs.

"For now, we are trying to track him down."

"You mean you don't have any info on him?"

The U.S. Marshall looked away. "We only recently discovered Anton had a son. There is no record of him, no paper trails."

Anguish spat on her insides. "How am I supposed to protect myself?"

He stood. "I can assure you will be protected."

"So where are you taking me? What's my new name and my disguise?"

He handed her another folder. "New Mexico. You're a librarian, married to a construction worker named Jake, and have a six-year-old daughter. Your new name is Lucy Mitchell."

"And don't worry about Jake. He too is part of the WITSEC program so he knows the drill," U.S. Marshall Adams said.

Staring at her new social security, driver's license, and passport, Dana flashed her heart-stopping smile, her disguise. Something burning crept inside her then burst out as laughter. It felt good to laugh after days of trauma.

The two U.S. Marshalls exchanged glances. She didn't care.

***

Agent Felicia placed a fax on Agent Kerry's desk. "Check out what the media's saying, that Dana Simmons has been spotted and just needed time to grieve her father's death."

Agent Wayne pushed the paper aside. "Heard about it on the news this morning. The WITSEC will have a difficult time pulling this off. She's famous, and it wouldn't be difficult to recognize her." He reached for the picture frame of his two daughters. Thank God they were safe. He wouldn't wish that to happen to them.

Felicia opened the window and stared out. "I feel bad for Rob Hanson. He's posted flyers on every block that she's missing. This is a man determined to find her."

He rustled the papers on his desk and punched a number on the phone. "He's attracting more attention to the mob. We need to keep a closer watch on him, you don't want the mob to harm him."

***

Flicking his cigarette, Rob was disgusted to learn from the news earlier that morning that Dana wasn't missing. The media indicated that tourists in France spotted her recuperating from the death of her father. That certainly didn't sound like Dana, and he didn't buy it.

He crossed the street, posted his last flyer, and entered Burt's cafe to meet the two FBI Agents.

Agent Wayne raised his hand. Rob approached the table and removed his leather jacket.

The waiter brought in coffee for the three of them.

"Thanks for coming to meet us in such short notice," Agent Wayne said.

"My lawyer doesn't want me speaking to you guys without him." He lit a cigarette. "But I've nothing to hide and I know something's not right. I'm her agent."

"We're aware of that." Agent Wayne said. "That's why we wanted to meet you."

Agent Raymond showed Rob the note from Dana's father.

Rob read the note, his breathing becoming more ragged.

"Is everything all right?"

Rob bit his lip. "The day Dana disappeared, she told me about this note."

"And why didn't you mention this to Officer Jones or Detective Schultz?"

Rob cracked his knuckles. "Dana told me this in confidence, and I thought if I mentioned this to the police, her life would be in danger."

"Her life already is in danger. You shouldn't withhold information from us."

Rob grabbed his jacket and stood. "My lawyer was right. I should have never come here. You can't keep harassing me like I'm the bad guy here. You should be looking for the killer of those four women."

"Wait." Agent Raymond held up her hand. "Please seat down. We aren't here to accuse you."

"We want to help you, and maybe you can *help* us too," Agent Wayne added.

Furrowing his eyebrows, Rob plopped himself onto the chair. "I hope this isn't some plot to frame me."

Agent Wayne continued, "We know you're in a difficult situation, but we need somebody determined like you."

"We believe the kidnapping of Stacy Kestav is connected to the four women who were murdered and also to your friend, Dana Simmons."

Rob straightened his shoulders, relieved. "Thank you. That's what I've been trying to say all this time, but nobody listens to me."

***

Vladimir Marcovic watched the three monitors in his office, the video of young women engaging in sex. Shifting his gaze to his father's portrait that hung on the wall triggered a distant memory when he was six years old.

"Come here, Vladimir," His father had pulled him to sit on his lap as they sat in the restaurant they owned. Nobody was there except for a lady singer auditioning. "Isn't she beautiful?" His eyes had beamed in admiration. "When you grow up, you need to find a woman like that."

"I want someone like Mommy," Vladimir said.

His father grinned. "Mommy's okay, too simple. But this woman is the bomb. You need women like that."

Vladimir nodded.

The door flung open, and a group of young women flooded in and threw themselves at his father. They ordered drinks, lit cigarettes, and smoked away.

"Slow down, ladies." His father chuckled. "My son's here."

The ladies turned to Vladimir and tickled and kissed him till he couldn't stop laughing.

On their way home, Vladimir had spotted his mother outside the porch waiting for them. She cursed her father in Russian.

He leaned his body against hers. "I'm making lots of money, why are you complaining?" His voice boomed and echoed as they entered their house.

"Other fathers play ball with their sons. It's not healthy to take him to your restaurant with all the smoke and women."

"You're comparing me to the husbands of your friends? Well, most wives give their husbands children."

Vladimir had dashed to his room, but he could still hear his parents arguing. He learned he was adopted that day and hated his father ever since.

"All I'm saying is that why can't we be a normal family?"

"Who wants to be normal? Aren't you happy with all the money I give you? Don't you like this new house? How about the car? Do your friends have the clothes you have?"

"Stop it, Anton, stop it."

Vladimir turned on the TV, loud.

The door flung open, forcing Vladimir back to reality. He shook his head, clearing away the memory as his tall, suit-wearing cousin popped in.

"Constantine, what's up?"

"I thought you'd be interested to know that Stacy Kestav did her first act today."

Pursing his lips, he nodded. "Cool. Anything special about her?"

"Dude, I had to test her first." He licked his lips like a vampire who just sucked blood.

"I knew you would."

"What's the matter with you?" Constantine pulled out a chair and sat across from him. "You don't seem happy. Our viewers have doubled on the site, and the men here love our Russian women."

"Same shit, different day, Constantine." He sighed. "I've been doing this as far as I can remember."

"I'm new to all this, and I love it." Constantine put his feet on Vladimir's desk and shifted his gaze to the Central Park out the window. "We have a beautiful building with an amazing view, women at our beck and call, and money flowing out of our ears. Man, this is the *life*."

Vladimir didn't blink as he remembered his father's exact words: "The Marcovic family possesses power and prestige. We will evolve through generations and become more powerful than we can ever imagine."

"Okay, grouch, I'll leave you to your peace. I'll get you your favorite mango parfait from Ginny's Delights. That should cheer you up." He stood and exited the room.

Vladimir rolled his eyes.

Vladimir opened the drawer and removed his father's letter which he gave before he died.

> *Dear Vladimir,*
>
> *I know I wasn't the father you expected me to be, and I blame myself for all my mistakes. You're a good son, and I'm entrusting the business to you. My only request is that you find Marcy Simmons and the daughter I never met and keep them safe.*
>
> *Love,*
> *Dad*

Vladimir banged his hand on his desk. *Even on your deathbed, all you cared about was Marcy. I found Marcy, Dad, and I will find your dear daughter, and when I do, I'll kill them both.*

Chapter 14

Dana stood at the doorstep of Jake Mitchell's home, clutching an overnight bag with six sets of clothing she never would have dared to wear before.

U.S. Marshall Collins stood beside her, dressed casually in jeans and a t-shirt. "Remember, you are to confide in nobody." He tucked a cell phone inside her purse. "I'm on speed dial one. Don't call your friends. This phone is only for emergency."

Dana rolled her eyes. "I get it. What makes you think I'd want to use that cell phone when it's not a smart phone."

U.S. Marshall Collins raised his eyebrows. "Precisely."

Dana clutched her hair. Far too short. Gone were her long blond locks. Dyed jet black now. She didn't even recognize herself. Tugging her jumper, cursing under her breath despite her life being in danger. Not giving in to her shallow pursuits, Dana couldn't help but feel like she was in dire need of a fashion emergency. She reached inside her pocket and clutched the locket necklace. There was no way U.S Marshall Collins would take that away from her.

A little girl peered from inside the window and waved her tiny hand.

A sweaty man with dark brown hair and a beard popped out the door. Dana and Jake locked gazes, and soon his stern look softened as he smiled.

"Jake Mitchell."

"Da—"

U.S. Marshall Collins cleared his throat. "This is Lucy."

"Please to meet you." Jake clutched her hand tight.

Dana swallowed hard, noting Jake's filthy nails. She turned to U.S. Marshall Collins.

"Sorry." Jake pulled his hand away. "The construction site has been cruel to my nails. Do come in."

U.S. Marshall Collins stayed put. "I gotta run. Lucy knows where to reach me."

Jake nodded and escorted Dana inside.

A cold shiver ran through Dana's spine as she stood in the hallway. She couldn't bring herself to take another step when she glanced at the yellow wallpaper. *Is this a joke?* To her left was the living room with same boxed TV she had while growing up. Dana overheard the cartoon show and saw the little girl lying on her stomach with eyes glued to the TV. She felt like she was revisiting memory lane, but this time, Dana was the outsider.

"I won't bite," Jake said.

"Sorry."

The little girl approached them and clutched Dana's hand. Dana froze when the little girl tugged her arm.

"What's your name?" Dana asked following the little girl and sat beside her, the girl curling up beside her.

Jake watched them from the hallway. "She's deaf."

Dana broke into a sweat. "I'm sorry."

He approached them in the living room. "My wife died during childbirth. Molly was born this way."

He still wore his wedding ring, and it brought back memories of her father. Dana had thought coming to New York would help her forget her past, yet here she was confronted with the reality she couldn't escape.

"I'm sorry." Digging in her pockets, she put on her faux wedding ring that U.S. Marshall Collins gave her earlier that day.

Jake shrugged. He faced Molly and while talking, made a sign that time was up and she needed to get ready for bed.

Molly pouted and held her hand up.

"All right, but only five more minutes." Jake turned to Dana. "Let me show you upstairs."

Dana trailed behind him, and they entered the master's bedroom. A humble queen-sized bed with no decorations occupied the room. Her heart sank like a deflated balloon when she glanced at the bare closet.

"This is where you'll be staying." Jake muttered. "I'll sleep on the floor."

"Thank you." Dana laid her bag on the corner and sat on the bed. It sank down. She'd now be sharing a room with a stranger who didn't even look at her. Dana had been used to men gawking and ogling her like a goddess, and she had to admit that she enjoyed the attention. But today, she felt that she was below ordinary. U.S. Marshall Collins and Adams would compliment her for the perfect disguise.

"There are fresh towels in the bathroom. I'm usually out at five. Our neighbor, Rachel, takes Molly to school every day. She's usually here at six and helps Molly get ready, but perhaps, tomorrow you can…"

"I can help her get ready and cook breakfast." Dana surprised herself saying that. Since when did she cook anybody breakfast? Breakfast for her was fresh fruit, but she knew Molly would prefer bacon and eggs or even pancakes.

"I made a list of things that Molly likes," he added.

She nodded, meeting his eyes and capturing the tenderness and pain he felt. Consumed with her own problems, Dana never asked U.S. Marshall Collins and Adams why Jake was part of the WITSEC.

"Thank you." He removed his shoes and set them aside. "Listen, please don't feel obliged to do this. I don't want you to think I'm doing you a favor. I can only imagine how difficult this may be for you, but your secret is safe with me."

Dana looked away. She thought of her mother living from state to state, trying to blend in like a chameleon, never knowing when she would be free. "What did you tell Molly about me?"

He grinned. "My daughter may be six, but she's quite sharp. I told her Daddy has a new wife who will be living with us."

Dana pursed her lips. "Were your friends surprised that you got married?"

"Sort of." He smirked. "I gotta tuck Molly to sleep. Feel at home, Lucy." He left her alone with her thoughts.

Dana pulled out her cell phone, contemplating if she should call Rob, but decided against it. She took the envelope and counted her money—enough to buy a beat-up car to get to work.

Perhaps she could imagine that she was on a vacation, that this was only temporary. Her ultimate goal was to save her mother and to track down Vladimir Marcovic so she could kill him.

Chapter 15

In one week, Dana had bought a Beetle, settled into her job at the library, and bonded with Molly. She even picked up a book on sign language.

Dana was frustrated to live in a small town like Blue Acres, New Mexico. Her research showed that only two hundred and six people lived there, and everybody seemed to be clannish. Nobody paid her any attention at the library, and the silence allowed her to spend time mapping out her escape. Each day, U.S. Marshall Collins checked up on her via phone like a guard checked on his prisoners. That's what she was—a prisoner with an identity crisis.

Today, she had visited the local grocery and almost asked the cashier if they sold organic produce. Instead, she bought fresh vegetables, vowing to introduce healthy eating for Jake and Molly. She was tired of the frozen pot roast and mashed potatoes Jake served for dinner, and she was thrilled when she found quinoa.

Dana slipped out of her car and opened the trunk to pick up her grocery bags. As she closed the trunk, she froze as a man smoking a cigarette stood in front of her. "You scared me. Can I help you?"

His dark eyes settled on her. "You know where the nearest gas station is?"

She avoided eye contact and pointed south. "Two blocks, make a right on the first street. You'll find a gasoline station at the corner."

He flicked his cigarette to the ground and went back to his pickup truck. "Thank you." His tires screeched as he drove off.

Dana caught her breath, her heart still pounding.

Rachel and Molly appeared moments later. Molly gave Dana a tight embrace and held out a picture of two dolphins. Rachel planted her hands stubbornly on her heavy hips while her plunging breasts looked like they were going to explode from her blouse.

Dana wished she could take the lady shopping. She placed her hands on her chest to show how much she loved Molly's drawing. Facing Rachel, she said. "You guys came home early today."

Rachel furrowed her eyebrows. "Tuesdays and Thursdays are early release days. Didn't you look at the calendar posted on the refrigerator?"

"Right." *What a bitch!*

"What's the matter with you? You look like you saw a ghost." Rachel peered inside the grocery bags. "What's all this? Is this what you're feeding Jake?" She shook her head. "Oh, let me tell you, he works hard at the construction site and this ain't going to feel him up."

With one hand holding Molly and the other hand carrying the grocery bags, Dana gave Rachel her heart-stopping smile. "Oh, Rachel, I don't know about you, but in our home, we like to spice things up. Didn't Jake tell you about Thursday nights?" She paused. "Oh right, I should remind you that Thursday nights are when we try a new recipe. Perhaps I can write it down for you. Would you like a magnet calendar for that?"

Rachel glared at her.

Serves her right!

***

Dana sipped her wine. Jake politely chewed two bites of the eggplant casserole she made and barely touched the quinoa. Molly stared at the food and refused to eat.

Dana exited to the kitchen and pulled out a box of Mac and cheese and French bread from the cupboard.

As she prepared the food, Jake squeezed her shoulders, touching her for the first time since they shook hands. "I'm sorry."

"It's all right." She put pressure on the bread knife as she sliced the bread into small pieces.

Jake rested his hands on hers. "Let me."

She watched his strong hands slice the bread and noticed how clean his fingernails were. They locked gazes. He flashed her a comforting smile, like the one her father used to give her mother when they would sit at the backyard during the summer listening to The Beatles song, *Yesterday*. It was her dad's way of telling her he would take care of her.

After dinner, Molly leaned her head on Dana's shoulder while they watched *SpongeBob*

SquarePants, Jake sitting beside them on the couch. Soon, Molly dozed off.

Dana broke the silence. "Jake, can I ask you a personal question?"

He grunted. "Yeah, sure."

"Did you see anyone after your wife died?"

He didn't answer.

Dana faced him. "I know you had something with Rachel."

His eyes open wide. "Who told you that?"

Dana crossed her legs, convinced that Jake and Rachel had an affair.

"It happened only once. I needed someone to comfort me, and one thing led to another and then we were in bed." His eyes averted to the TV.

"Why didn't you make it official? She seems to act like she's Molly's mom."

He shook his head. "It wouldn't be fair to her since I don't feel the same way as she does. But she's a good friend to us."

"Trust me, she loves you," Dana said.

"What makes you say that?"

She shrugged.

"If Rachel is giving you a hard time, please let me know."

"Don't worry about me. I can take care of myself." She smiled at him."Does it get easier Jake?" She wanted to probe further about being part of the WITSEC, but decided against it.

Jake said, "As long as Molly and I are safe, I can't complain."

Jake had Molly and now she was a part of their family. She hoped to be a good mom to Molly but after losing her mom at ten, what example did she have?

***

Rob sat across Stanley's desk while his lawyer straightened his folders and pens. He had to inform Stanley about his plans and meeting with the FBI earlier that day. "Do you always need to do that?"

"I can't work with a messy desk." He leaned forward. "Now where were we?"

"Something ain't right. I don't believe Dana's in Europe. Did you talk to the reporters? It's probably a crazy rumor to divert attention. They still haven't found the killer of those four women. Rather suspicious, if you ask me, that they all were close to Dana's age and dress size. And how about Stacy's family?"

"Slow down. How many cups of coffee did you drink today? You look like you haven't had a full night's rest."

Rob sighed. He badly needed a drink or, better yet, a smoke. "I came here to tell you I'm leaving for Alaska tomorrow."

Stanley dropped his coffee and wet the folder. "Shit." He gathered paper napkins and wiped his desk.

"Sorry."

"What the hell are you going to do in Alaska?"

"I'll be assisting the FBI with their investigation.

"And you didn't bother consulting me about your plans?" Stanley gritted his teeth.

"Either way, I'm still going to look for Dana. They're on my side, and I need all the help I can get. I know Dana's alive, and I'll never stop looking for her."

"You don't know who you're dealing with, Rob, you need to be careful."

"Like I said, I came here to tell you that I'm leaving for Alaska first thing tomorrow."

***

Rob never dreamed of visiting Alaska, especially during the winter, but here he was, bundled in layers, shivering, and hoping the sun would rise like the morning dew and comfort him.

He stayed at a motel close to Dana's family home. He was glad she gave her address to him before she visited her father. Checking his wire, he whispered, "I'm here."

"Copy that," Agent Wayne said.

He threw his bag on the chair and pulled out a map. Rob needed to make sure he covered his tracks. Never in his wildest dreams did he ever think he would be helping the FBI, but this would bring him closer to solving Dana's disappearance. Both FBI agents gave him their word, and he was going to help them find Stacy Kestav.

One of his clients owned a private plane, and he'd been able to hitch a ride. He'd rent a car to drive back. Rob brought enough cash to last him for three days, maybe more.

Rob cocked his camera and unfolded the map of Anchorage. His motel was a mile away from Dana's house, and he had to think of a perfect excuse to go there.

***

At Ginny's Delights, Agents Kerry and Felicia sat across the table from Mrs. Kestav.

"This mango parfait is delicious." Felicia licked the tip of the spoon.

Mrs. Kestav gave her a soft smile. "Baking these pastries is no longer the same without Stacy." A tear shed from her eye. "I could still hear her humming while she baked. I hope they find the person who did this to her. She's a diabetic, you know. How will she survive without her insulin?"

"We're doing everything we can." Agent Wayne cleared his throat. "I'm sure you've seen the news about those four women?"

"Yes, and also about that model who is in Europe."

"That's correct," Felicia said. "Which means Stacy could still be alive."

Agent Wayne pushed a Paris brochure toward Mrs. Kestav. "You mentioned, Stacy wanted to move to Paris. Do you think she left ahead of schedule?"

The veins of Mrs. Kestav's neck tensed up. "We've been through this before. Stacy would never leave without saying goodbye. We are a close family."

Chapter 16

Dana glanced at her watch. Three more minutes until the library closed. Dana wondered how Rob was and wished she could reach out to him. She hated that he was trapped in the spider's web like she was. Averting her gaze to her fellow librarian locking up, she said, "Hey, Sarah, just wanted to ask you if you know of a good clothing store aside from the Goodwill store in the area."

Sarah eyed Dana's floral dress. "Where did you say you were from again?"

Dana sighed. "Orlando, Florida."

"Right." Sarah stacked books in a cart. "It must be difficult for you to adjust in this small town, but there's always online shopping."

A smile spread across Dana's face. "Why didn't I think of that?" But then she frowned. U.S. Marshall Collins had said no calls, no social media, no texting or online chats. *Hmmm, does shopping count?* Perhaps it wouldn't hurt if she ordered just one dress. She was tired of wearing floral pastels. Surely vamping up her attire would make her feel better.

A male customer with a thick beard entered the library.

Sarah studied him. "I'm sorry, but we're closing."

"I'll only be a moment."

Facing Dana, Sarah asked, "Do you think you can help this gentleman? Dave and I have a Bible study meeting to go to."

Dana approached the counter. "Sure, you go ahead. I'll take care of it." Then toward the man, she asked, "What can I help you with?" She opened the log book.

He picked up a pen and signed his name. "I'm looking for a book for a seven-year-old."

"Oh, a child. You'll find books on the second shelf to your left."

"Here's the thing." He scratched his chin, avoiding her gaze. "She's deaf."

"Oh." *What a coincidence.* Dana marched around the counter and toward the shelves. "Deaf children can still read books like other kids, but I think she would like—"

"She wants me to borrow the Harry Potter books, but I'm not sure that's appropriate for her age." He shrugged. "She said she read the first book in two days."

"Wow! She must be a prolific reader." Dana removed the Harry Potter books from the shelf and walked back to the counter.

"She never ceases to surprise me. Her teacher said I need to continue stimulating her mind. Otherwise she gets bored."

Dana scanned the bar codes and placed the books inside a bag. "I know what you mean. My step-daughter is deaf too."

He was taken aback. "No kidding. Where does she go to school?"

"Bernard's." She caught her breath. U.S. Marshall Collins had said not to divulge any information to strangers.

"She must know my daughter. What's her name?"

For a moment, Dana hesitated but then said, "Molly... Molly Mitchell."

"Oh, right, Jake Mitchell's daughter." He showed her his library card. "I'm Pete Glascow. I didn't know Jake remarried."

Dana's cheeks flushed. "I'm Da—I mean Lucy."

Pete took the bag of books. "Well, it was nice meeting you, Lucy. I don't want to keep you, but you have a good evening."

"You too, thanks." Dana had to keep reminding herself she lived in a small town now.

***

After she finished up at the library, Dana returned home and entered with a bag of books.

Rachel glared at her from the hallway. "You're late. I already fed and bathe Molly."

Molly dashed toward Dana and gave her a tight embrace. Ignoring Rachel, Dana bent down and showed her the Harry Potter books. A smile was now plastered in Molly's lips as she pulled Dana to the couch.

Rachel trailed behind them. "Harry Potter? You know those books are too matured for her. She's six years old."

Molly flipped through the pages of the books.

"I wonder if Jake will approve of this."

Dana faced her. "You listen to me, Rachel. Not once have I snapped at you because I know you were a good friend of Jake's previous wife, but today I'm going to tell you that I don't appreciate how you treat me. Beginning tomorrow, I will take Molly to school and pick her up as well. I will be the one to feed and bathe her."

"But Jake said—"

"Jake and I are together, and this is my house, which means I get to decide how I want to handle this situation."

Rachel stormed out of the house, murmuring, "I knew it. Jake made a big mistake."

Dana followed her outside. "Really? I wonder why Jake never pursued a relationship with you."

Rachel's jaw dropped. "You bitch."

Dana gave her a heart-stopping smile. Jake's car pulled up to the curb, and she dashed toward him and kissed him on the lips. "Oh, honey, I'm so glad you're home. You don't know how much I missed you."

Jake awkwardly embraced her as Rachel watched.

Rachel shook her head. "You're making a big mistake, Jake. This woman is no good for you."

Jake held up his hand. "Rachel, I appreciate all that you've done for Molly and I, but I will not allow you to insult Lucy." He squeezed Lucy's hand. "Honey, let's go inside."

Dana flashed Rachel one last smile before retreating inside. They shut the door, and the three of them settled in the couch.

"I'm sorry about Rachel." Dana swallowed. "She's been rude to me all this time, and I told her that beginning tomorrow, I will be the one to take Molly to school."

"What about your job?"

"Molly is more important."

Molly showed him the library books.

"Harry Potter?"

"Pete Glascow's daughter borrowed a set as well at the library today for his daughter, and I thought why can't I have Molly read them too?"

"Makes sense. Thank you." He gave her that tender look.

Jake was a keeper. No doubting that.

***

Rob surveyed the humble two-story waterfront home surrounded by tall pine trees, no neighbors in sight. There was an old-fashioned mailbox, and a fishing boat with two fishing rods sat on the dock. He brushed snow from his jacket and snapped photos. Looking around to make sure nobody was watching, Rob slashed the two tires of the rented Range Rover. He whispered to the wired mic. "Wish me luck."

"We have your back. Be careful," Agent Wayne said.

He smirked as he approached the door and rang the bell. *So this is where Dana grew up.*

A man in his mid-forties opened the door. "Can I help you?"

Removing his beanie, Rob caught his breath. "Sorry to bother you. I'm David. I was taking a hike only to discover that somebody slashed my tires. Do you think you can give me a hand?"

The man scrutinized him from head to toe. "Michael. Let me get my tools." He disappeared and came back moments later with a wrench and a black bag.

The men worked on replacing the tires.

"Nice place you got here," Rob nodded toward the lake.

"Yeah, I bought it for a quite a steal." Michael grinned. "Very unusual for your tires to get slit. This place is pretty safe."

"I was surprise myself."

He eyed the plate number. "Seattle? How long was the drive?"

"Three days, max. I stopped to get food and sleep in between. It's a good scenic route, but I should have done this during the summer."

Tightening the screw, Michael said, "I'll be experiencing my first summer this year. I'm so looking forward to fishing."

Rob glanced at the boat. "Where did you move from?"

"Upstate New York. Still have my house there, but looks like I'll be spending more time here. How about you? What do you do?"

"I'm a real estate broker. I'm trying to expand my network."

"Really? Do you have a card?"

Rob pretended to look in his wallet. "Shoot. Looks like I ran out, but if you give me one of yours, I can email you."

Digging into his pocket, Michael plucked out a business card and handed it to Rob.

Rob studied the card. "A boat dealer. Wow. Never met one before."

Michael grinned. "It's pretty neat."

"Hey, thanks for helping me out. Do you think I can use your restroom before I leave?"

"Sure. As soon as you enter, make a right and you'll see the bathroom."

Rob stepped inside the house. The inside looked surprisingly modern compared to the outside. He pulled out his digital camera to snap photos real quick.

After they exchanged goodbyes, Rob hopped into the Range Rover and sped away. To the mic, he said, "I didn't see anything unusual, but that doesn't mean anything."

"How does he look?" Felicia asked.

"Seems like a charming man, mid-forties, brown hair, average height and built. He can blend in with a crowd."

"Thanks for cooperating with us, Rob," Agent Wayne said. "We'll let you know if we have any latest developments."

"A pleasure working with you, but like I said, I won't stop searching for Dana."

***

Kerry took a sip of water while Felicia peered out the window, which overlooked Michael Downey's house.

"Remind me again why we're at this dingy motel?" She asked.

Kerry mumbled, "If we find more clues about Downey, we can catch the next plane outta here. That will teach you to pack light."

"Yeah, yeah. Didn't Rob say there weren't any clues?"

Kerry groaned. "We need to double check."

Kerry and Felicia stepped out of the rented Corolla across Sarah Winter's house.

"Are you sure you got the right address?" Kerry asked.

"For the tenth time, when are you going to stop asking me that?" Felicia rolled her eyes.

"All right, I'll just let you do the talking."

Felicia skipped up the steps and rang the doorbell of the house down the street from Michael Downey.

A plump lady with dark hair popped outside. "Can I help you?"

"My brother and I are here for a wedding of Sheila Downey." Felicia paused. "We just got in from California, and we're not sure we have the right address."

Looking above, the woman said, "Not sure about a Sheila Downey, but we do have a new neighbor named Michael Downey who lives right there." She gestured her hand.

Felicia followed her gaze. "Looks pretty empty to me."

She shrugged. "I never met him. Seems to keep to himself all the time."

"Really? You don't think he's related to Sheila?" Kerry interjected.

"I'm not sure, and I don't think anyone is home." She stepped inside her home then came back with a bunch of letters. "Would you be so kind enough to do me a favor?"

"Sure," Felicia said.

"Can you give these to him? The mailman dropped them here by mistake."

"Sure," Felicia said and bid her goodbye. "She went over the mail."

They walked back to the Corolla and climbed inside.

Felicia made a face. "What is it with people from small towns? Why are they so trusting?"

"Tell me about it." Kerry cleared his throat. "What if we were serial killers?"

"Should we knock at his house?"

"Let's try the other neighbors."

The agents walked to other side of the road and knocked on the door of the home on the corner.

A clean-shaven man with wind-swept hair greeted them. "Can I help you?"

"Oh, hi, you must be..." Felicia paused, as if gathering her thoughts. "We're looking for our cousin Sheila Downey. I'm not sure we got the right address."

The man studied them. "Don't know anybody by that name."

"Is this Twenty-One Cauliflower Street?" Kerry asked.

"It's the third house on your left."

"Do you know her?"

The man huffed. "Who are you, the cops?"

"We're going now." Kerry tugged Felicia. "Have a nice day."

As the two agents trotted down the street, Felicia asked, "How many more houses do we have to knock in?"

"One, his."

They surveyed the lakefront property. Kerry rang the doorbell and waited. When nobody came out, he tucked in the letters underneath the doorstep.

"Looks like his neighbor is right, Michael doesn't seem to be around."

***

Vladimir watched the man and woman leave letters underneath his doorstep and waited until they left to make a call.

"How's my favorite cousin?" Constantine asked in his cheery voice.

"Listen, I need you to check on this guy, David Benson, a realtor from Seattle."

"Are you planning to buy property there?"

Vladimir eyed the business card. "Nope, he appeared on my driveway. Slashed tire."

"Let me guess. You helped him."

"Too obvious if I didn't."

"Okay, will check on him. Is that all you need?"

He leaned toward the window. "Order me a hidden camera. The street has been busy lately."

"Right on."

Fuck!

Chapter 17

Three months had passed since Dana moved to Albuquerque and she was finally getting used to her new life. While the library patrons were busy reading books, Dana surfed the internet. She typed in "Vla" then backspaced. How will she be able to find Vladimir if she didn't know where to look?

An ad for her favorite retail shop that sold black and white clothing flashed on the screen. Her mouth watered. If only she could buy a dress or two. Jake didn't make her pay anything at home with her humble salary and now that she left earlier than usual to pick up Molly from school, there was no way she could afford to buy these extravagant dresses.

But she did have her debit card number memorized. She clenched her hands as temptation tugged her intestines. Should she buy it?

What's one dress? She accessed the Bank of America website and typed in her username and password. Her jaw dropped. *Why do I have more money than I had? Oh... The sale of Dad's house.* She switched back to the online shopping site and went on a shopping spree.

Sarah nudged her from behind. "So, you took my advice seriously."

Dana lunged her hand on her chest. "You scared me."

"I'm sorry."

Contemplating between pressing the purchase button, Dana stared at the screen.

"C'mon, buy it," Sarah dared. "You deserve it, you know that."

Flashing her a sheepish grin, Dana said, "I don't think I should."

"Silly, if you don't do it, I'll buy them for you."

Dana tapped Sarah's hand. "You don't need to do that for me."

"I insist."

"Sh." Dana placed her finger on her mouth as the patrons glanced at them.

Sarah whispered, "If you're scared that Jake will think you're overspending, you can have it delivered to my house and I can tell Jake I gave it to you." She winked.

A smile spread across Dana's lips. Little did Sarah know that Dana had bigger problems than that, but Sarah's solution seemed great. She needed to find a way to get her money and blamed herself for failing to discuss this with U.S. Marshall Collins and Adams. Her *hard-earned* money. "Sarah, you don't know how much that means to me. I will take your offer."

"Sure thing. I'll let you know when the package arrives."

***

After work, Dana lined up at the bank. As she reached the clerk, she handed over the check.

"Can I see your ID, Lucy?"

Digging inside her purse, she pulled out her fake driver's license and gave it to the clerk.

The clerk glanced at it and looked up at her. "Would you like to open an account with us? It will save you the trouble of—"

"That's all right. Can you please give me the cash?"

"Sure. You want them in twenties or hundreds?"

"Hundreds should be fine." She sighed. The cash she had was only one-tenth of what she really owned and she was looking forward to the clothes she ordered. Surely, U.S. Marshall Collins hadn't realized what these outdated clothes were doing to her self-esteem.

***

Jake stepped inside the house, holding a paper bag, while Dana and Molly were curled up on the couch watching cartoons that evening.

"You're early," Dana said.

"Thought I'd surprise you both. Let's go out to dinner tonight." He arched her a smile.

Molly insisted he carry her piggyback. He laid the bag on the couch and ran around the living room while Molly giggled. Moments like this got her all misty-eyed. She missed her father so much. She appreciated him more now that he protected her back then and wished she had visited him more often before he died.

Jake bent down and released Molly. She continued to laugh as she smudged her nose against his.

"Daddy has to take a shower. Then we'll go to dinner at your favorite restaurant," he said and signed. Jake picked up the paper bag and pulled out a pink dress. "So you can wear this new dress."

Molly gave him a huge embrace then swirled around the living room, holding her dress.

Dana watched them in delight.

Locking eyes with Dana, Jake plucked out another dress and gave it to her. "I figured you were a size zero, but wasn't sure. We can return it in case you don't like it."

Dana studied the black and white dress and welled up in tears. "It's beautiful. Thank you. And yes it fits." *How could he possibly know black and white are my favorite colors?* She kissed him on the cheek.

Silence crossed between them before he said, "Let me take a quick shower so we can go."

She nodded, wiping the tears from her face. *How thoughtful of him. Maybe I shouldn't have gone on a shopping spree.*

Jake excused himself while Dana tidied up the house. Molly had rushed to her room with her dress.

***

At the Italian restaurant, Dana twirled her spaghetti in silence. Wearing the dress Jake gave her made her feel beautiful again, something she hadn't felt in months. Her hair had grown a little bit above her shoulder, and some patrons threw her admiring glances. However, she was surprised Jake had shaved his beard. His eyes spelled gentleness and the sacrifice and love he bestowed his daughter melted her heart. But she couldn't get too close. This was only temporary till she got her old life back.

Her thoughts drifted back to her glamorous life on the catwalk. She missed the makeup artists polishing her face while the hair stylist worked wonders on her hair. When was the last time she got a manicure and pedicure done? Perhaps she would convince Sarah to have a girls' day out.

"Lucy, you okay?"

She morphed back into reality. "Yeah. Sorry."

"Is your food okay?" He eyed her spaghetti.

"Yeah, it's good."

"You haven't touched it."

She plunged the fork inside her mouth and chewed. "It's really good."

Molly was oblivious to them both as she colored while chewing her pizza.

Dana reached for her glass in time for Jake to rest his hand on hers. "I want you to be happy," he said.

She steadied her gaze then drank water. "Thank you."

From the corner of her eye, Dana spotted a tall man with a leather jacket looking toward them. She blinked. *This guy looks familiar. Where have I seen him before?*

The man followed the waiter escorting him to a table.

Jake snapped his fingers. "Lucy."

"Oh, sorry." She flinched.

"Are you ready to go?"

"Sure." She took Molly's hand, and they exited the restaurant.

***

"Look at this, Vladimir," Towering high, Constantine looked down at him and pointed on the computer screen as he typed in codes. "Someone from New Mexico went on a shopping spree."

Vladimir fixed his glasses and bent down to check. "Now look at that, you hacker."

"Yeah. The press is making it appear that Dana Simmons is traveling in Europe, but somebody ordered clothes from The Black and White shop..." He Googled Dana Simmons. Images of the supermodel flashed on the screen. "Voila, this woman loves black and white."

Vladimir rubbed his chin. "Could be a coincidence."

"A coincidence? I don't think so. Do you think a supermodel like Dana could survive in a small town in New Mexico?"

Vladimir smirked. "Could be someone else trying to provide a distraction."

"What's the matter with you? You don't seem interested in finding her."

"Well, I could make some calls in their town and try to get him some leads."

Constantine glared at him. "You know that ain't a good idea. We need to do these ourselves. You can't be too obvious."

Vladimir took a big gulp of his coffee. "I understand how aggressive you can be since it's only your first year in the business. Wait until you reach twenty years, and you'll think it's the same shit and just another day."

He put his fingers to his eyes then pointed at him. "Well, that's why you need someone like me. Fresh eyes, eager like a lion, ready to gobble up his prey."

Vladimir chuckled. "What do you propose?"

Constantine leaned his hip on his desk. "I believe we should do this in our own time." He tossed brochures of Albuquerque New Mexico on his desk. "We're both due for a vacation."

Vladimir shook his head. "That's my territory now. Get back to work."

Scowling, Constantine left the room.

From above the rim of his glasses, Vladimir studied the purchases then grinned.

His phone rang. "Yep."

"I believe I found your girl," the caller said in a smooth voice. "I wasn't sure the first time, but saw her again at the Italian restaurant wearing a black dress and she sure looked like the photo you gave me."

"Good job. I'll make sure you get a bonus, Ted." He hanged up and punched in a number.

"Thank you for calling Seasons Travel. How may I direct your call?"

"I need a one way ticket to New Mexico from Anchorage."

"Where in New Mexico, sir?"

"Bluewater Acres." He diverted his gaze outside the window, watching snowflakes fall into the ground. A wicked smile spread across his lips as he imagined what he would do to Dana once he saw her.

The clicking sound of the computer keys overshadowed his thoughts. "You'll need to fly to Albuquerque, and it's about a hundred twenty miles to get to—"

"When is the next flight?"

"Would you prefer a layover in LAX or Arizona?"

"It doesn't matter, just book me the damn flight." He took off his glasses and removed his wallet from his pocket.

"Okay, sir." He overheard typing on a keyboard. "I have one flight leaving at noon and—"

"I'll take that." He gave her his credit card info and waited for her to transmit the confirmation then hanged up. Rubbing his hands together, he grinned. "Dana Simmons, we will finally meet."

Chapter 18

Dana was delighted when Sarah showed up at her doorstep and embraced her tight. "You came."

"And I'm early," Sarah said. "Oh, and your package is going to arrive tomorrow."

Swirling around, she burst into a smile. "Yippee." A surge of adrenaline sprinkled upon Dana.

As they climbed into Dana's Beetle, Sarah nudged Dana. Rachel was watching them from her window. "Look how much she envies you."

Dana started the ignition then backed up from the driveway. "Don't pay attention to her. She's a miserable woman."

"Oh, those are the ones you need to *pay attention* to since you don't know what they're capable of."

Shifting gears, Dana stepped on the gas and turned on the radio. "Let's not worry about that today. I can't wait to get my nails done and have a facial."

Sarah grinned. "Same here. I think we should do this once a quarter."

Tapping on her steering wheel, Dana blurted, "Are you kidding me? I used to get mine done once a week."

"Seriously?" Sarah arched her eyebrows. "You sound like a spoiled supermodel," she laughed.

Swallowing hard, Dana remembered she was *Lucy the librarian,* not *Dana the supermodel.*

"You okay?"

"Yeah." She blinked. "Of course, I'm no supermodel. What I meant was my fantasy would be to have a spa day every week and not worry about cooking, cleaning, laundry, you know... the works."

"Oh, I hear you." Sarah snapped her fingers. "That would be paradise."

Yeah, paradise.

***

Constantine rolled his suitcase outside the airport as Vladimir shook his head. The moon hid beneath the clouds while they strolled to their rented Ford Mustang.

"Remind me again why you needed to come with me?" Vladimir lighted a cigarette.

His cousin plucked the cigarette from his lips. "If you want to concentrate on finding your supermodel, you better quit smoking."

Vladimir combed his fingers through his hair, "You're worst than my mother."

Constantine winked. The cab driver pulled up to the curb then stepped down to put their luggage inside the trunk.

"I don't know why you never learned the art of packing light," Vladimir groaned.

His cousin chuckled. "What would you do without me?"

He smirked and climbed into the car.

"Cheer up," Constantine said. "I got us tickets to the balloon museum and the old town as well. We might find her there."

"You're going to drain me."

"On the contrary, I'm going to inject some life into you." Constantine laughed. "Have you forgotten that public places are the most convenient locations to commit a crime?"

But Vladimir was wishing he came alone. His younger cousin could be hasty, and his greed often consumed him.

***

Dana and Sarah giggled as they marched back to the car, their nails shimmering against the sun.

Sarah slurped her iced tea and beamed. "I feel like a queen today."

"And we shall rule the kingdom, Queen Sarah," Dana added while she shut the door of her Beetle.

"I wonder what Jake is going to say when he sees you. You're such a lucky woman to be with him. When his wife died, the single women of Bluewater Acres threw themselves at him, but he spent time raising his daughter."

Dana didn't flinch, she kept her eyes on the road. "I guess I'm lucky."

"How did you two meet anyway?"

Biting her lip, Dana gathered her thoughts. She had to replay the game of charades Agent Collins prepped her. "Um, nothing extraordinary. I was in the area and asked him for directions at the gasoline station."

"Really? What were you doing here?"

Heart pounding, Dana opened the window.

"I mean, I don't know anyone who wants to come to Bluewater Acres."

"I was lost. A friend and I went to Albuquerque for a wedding, and we made the wrong left turn. My friend dared me to ask him out so I gave him my number." She winked, fascinated by how natural a fabricated story could be. "I didn't think he'd call, but I'm glad he did."

"Wow, and who says that ain't extraordinary? Oh, girl, that's better than my story. Ask me how I met Jim."

"How?"

"We were neighbors and walked to school together every day. I hated his guts until one day he kissed me." Sarah giggled, and Dana glanced over to see a tainted blush spread on her face. "And I thought he could be cool."

Swerving to the right, Dana laughed. "A kiss can change everything."

"Tell me about it. I was love-struck after that day. I couldn't even look at him, and he thought I got angry that he kissed me."

"Boys." Dana sighed. "They can be so clueless at times." Her thoughts shifted to Jake, probably the only man who didn't seem clueless. But she had to remind herself not to get too close.

***

Vladimir waited in his car rental, staring at Sarah Winter's house. He let Constantine visit the balloon museum by himself. This had to be done alone. The white picket fence surrounded by pink roses gave light to the faded paint of the ranch-style home. Vladimir had surveyed the area earlier that afternoon, and nobody was home except for the golden retriever that slept on the front lawn.

Glancing at his watch, Vladimir turned on the timer and gave a wry smile.

Moments later, a UPS truck pulled over the curb. A man slipped out of the car carrying a box.

Scrutinizing the area, Vladimir bolted out of his car and approached him.

The driver greeted him. "I'm looking for Sarah Winters."

"Let me take that for my wife. She needs to stop shopping. When I told her that her clothes can't fit inside her closet, she asked me if she can have mine." He shared a laugh with the driver.

"My wife is the same. She claims she has nothing to wear when she has outfits she's never touched." He handed Vladimir the delivery receipt for his signature.

Vladimir signed Jim Winters' name. "Thanks."

The driver jumped in his delivery truck and rolled down the window. "I hope she doesn't return the items and order again," he chuckled.

"They always find the perfect excuse to buy more clothes."

"Tell me about it." The driver waved and sped off.

Clutching the box, Vladimir strode to his car and laid it on the passenger seat while he waited. "Oh, you poor supermodel. You just couldn't resist splurging on stylish outfits."

He stripped the tape and pulled out four black and white dresses. Closing his eyes, he sniffed the clothing and imagined what it would be like to undress Dana Simmons. He couldn't deny she was gorgeous.

A car drove by, and he snapped back to reality.

He was about to go down, when his cell phone rang. "Yeah."

A man with a raspy voice spoke. "That real estate guy you were telling me about from Seattle doesn't exist. Somebody's on the lookout for you."

Vladimir pressed his lips together. "I know."

"What are we going to do?"

"Like we always do. We blend in, remain calm, and do the merry-go-round." After a brief pause, he asked, "How's Marcy?"

"The usual."

He grinned. "I think you'll be interested to know that I found her daughter."

***

That morning, Dana still felt giddy after her spa day with Sarah. Dana cracked the eggs on the frying pan when the phone rang.

"Hey, Lucy, it's your lucky day. Your package arrived. Do you wanna swing by before going to work, or do you want me to take it with me to the library?"

Dana's heart leaped from her chest. "I thought it was going to arrive tomorrow. I'll be there in twenty minutes. I can't wait to try them on."

"I'll be waiting."

Humming, Dana hung up and set the table for three. She got the hang of serving bacon, eggs, and toast to Molly and Jake while she enjoyed fresh fruits. Dana sniffed the morning dew, knowing minutes from now she would be trying on new outfits. This was the highlight of her day—actually the highlight of her month.

A strange tune intruded her thoughts. Dana approached the counter where her purse laid and heard the faint sound again. She dug inside and removed her cell phone. Her heart went awry like spoiled broth as she flipped open the phone.

"What do you think you're doing ordering clothes from the Internet with your debit card?"

"I-I—"

"Meet me at the Shell gas station downtown in ten minutes." U.S. Marshall Collins raised his voice. "Leave everything behind and make sure nobody follows you."

"But-but—"

"Go."

After turning off the stove, Dana placed their breakfasts on Jake and Molly's plates. This was the last time she would cook for them. Tears cloaked her vision. Just when she was getting used to the way of life in this small town, it was stripped away from her.

She dashed outside the door and rushed to her Beetle. A glance behind revealed Rachel peeping. Dana had no time to think as she backed up from the driveway and drove to town.

U.S. Marshall Collins sat inside a beat down Jeep parked in the corner. Dana parked her car, climbed out, and rushed over. Head down, she stepped inside and ducked her head.

They didn't speak until they were miles away from Bluewater Acres.

"You put yourself at risk, Dana."

Dana refused to apologize. "I didn't come looking for trouble, and I didn't ask to live this way. All I ever wanted was freedom."

"There are other ways to handle this."

Oh how she hated U.S. Marshall Collins for stealing her life. What would Jake tell Molly when she woke up to discover that she was no longer there? This would be the second time Molly would lose a mother.

"Just so you know, your accounts have been frozen."

"But, that's my money," she yelled.

"Temporarily. I don't understand why you would put yourself at risk, Dana. I heard from Jake that you've been managing well, and now this?"

"You've been keeping tabs on me with Jake?" Dana glared at him. "I spoke to you every day."

U.S. Marshall Collins swerved through a curve, screeching his tires. "I needed to know you were okay. That's my job."

Dana stared out her window. How many other WITSEC victims felt the same way she did? It had more to do than playing disguise. They sabotaged her identity.

"I told you to call me if you need anything." He exited to the freeway.

"I know you have good intentions, but a man like you will never understand a woman's needs."

"Try me." He glanced at her. "I have a twin sister, and she's a girlie girl. For her birthday, I took her shopping and to the beauty salon."

Dana just shook her head.

"It's going to be okay." He patted her shoulder.

Dana forced a smile. She'd play the game. Maybe it would lead her closer to Vladimir. "Where are you taking me? I'm kinda getting used to this. I just have to remind myself not to get attached."

"Austin, Texas. Your name is Abigail Madison, and you manage a gift shop called Charmed and have one assistant."

Dana raised her eyebrow. "That sounds more like my type of job."

U.S. Marshall Collins handed her a bag. "I got you better clothes, a cinnamon shade of dye, and a map of Austin."

Dana peered inside and grinned at the retro orange shirt. "Pretty neat."

"And your social security, driver's license, and birth certificate."

"No shit. I should have been an actress so this game of charades would be easier for me."

"Oh, and you're very much single and live in the city. The shop is five minutes away."

"How very thoughtful of you, U.S. Marshall Collins." Dana's thoughts lingered on Jake and Molly. By now, they were up and wondering where she could be. And Sarah Winters waiting for her to show up so she could try on her new outfits. The students at the library who needed to have books checked out. Would she be missed? Did she make a difference in the few months that she lived there?

She eyed U.S. Marshall Collins, sleek as usual, doing his job as he promised, then imagined how difficult his job entailed protecting the innocent from the wicked. How many casualties suffered from all this? Dana promised herself she would

never be one of them. Convinced she had to find
Vladimir, and when Dana did, she would kill him.

Chapter 19

Vladimir sat at his dining table with seven other Russian men and rubbed his clean-shaven chin. "Dana Simmons escaped again."

"I don't know why you spend all your energy on this woman," Alex, a tall man with a scruffy beard said. "Business is doing well. We have doubled our viewers every month and raking in so much dough."

Vladimir stood and circled the table. "I need you to find the lady. Nobody is to question me why. I expect to hear feedback no later than Friday."

The men bowed their heads in silence.

"You're free to go," Vladimir added.

They dashed out from their seats and exited the premises while Vladimir retreated to his bedroom. Vladimir turned his queen-sized bed upside down to access his hidden stash of cash. After grabbing an overnight bag from his closet, he dumped the cash and clothes inside.

Now inside the bathroom, he applied shaving cream on his face, shaved. and washed his face. Gel in hands, he ran his fingers through his hair.

Pretending to hold a gun, Vladimir pointed toward the mirror then sky high, blowing air from his mouth.

Vladimir obtained daily reports about Marcy, but never had the courage to face here. He still considered her as the woman who stole the affection he longed from his father. She had been the apple of his father's eye. Even after years of her disappearance, his father still longed for her. She had destroyed his mother's life, his life, and she needed to pay for all she'd done.

***

Stacy Kestav's hope withered as, day in and out, she had been drugged, abused, and raped in front of the camera. Forced to pretend that she enjoyed the act despite losing her dignity, Stacy had enough. There were days when she could no longer cry, her heart too hollow from all the buried pain.

A man with gentle eyes unlocked her cell and took her hand. She had never seen this man before.

Yesterday she had been forced to act as a nun. Maybe today she'll be a nurse and the thought sickened her.

They climbed the stairs. The man unlocked the door and led her in a bedroom with no windows.

A beautiful woman with blond hair stood and straightened her skirt.

Oh no. He's one of those who likes to watch two women make out.

Removing her glasses, the woman asked, "Vladimir?"

He bowed his head. "She'll be rooming with you now." then left them and locked the door from the outside.

***

Vladimir dusted his hands. He didn't take one step away from the door when Constantine approached him. "What the hell are you doing putting Stacy with Marcy? Are you out of your mind?"

"Stacy's been through a lot. She doesn't need to be abused anymore."

"Somebody has a heart. You'd be surprised to know she's one of the favorites."

Vladimir marched down the hallway. "Look, Constantine, please stop questioning my decisions. You're still on my payroll and I can–"

"Yeah, boss me around like your father did to you. I'm still a Marcovic, you know that. You don't have to be a dick like your dad."

Whipping around, Vladimir held him on the throat. "Don't you ever tell me I'm like my father." He spat in his face. "I'm not." Releasing his hand, he drew in a breath and left Constantine gasping for air.

***

Stacy eyed the other woman and tucked a strand of her hair around her ear. "I'm Stacy Kestav."

The woman shook her hand giving her a tender look. "Marcy Simmons. Take a seat." She gestured toward the chair.

"I don't understand, why did they transfer me to this room?" Stacy took a seat opposite Marcy.

"When I was your age, I was a singer and worked in a club owned by Anton Marcovic. Little did I know that Anton was the leader of a Russian mob involved in human trafficking."

"Yes, they promised these Russian teens a better life here," Stacy chimed in. "I wonder how many of them there are."

"More than you can imagine," Marcy said. "Anton appeared to be a charming man. He gave me everything I ever wanted." Marcy bowed down. "The young and naive me agreed to be his mistress, not realizing the stakes involved."

Stacy listened intently not knowing anymore who to trust.

Marcy paced the room. "I thought he only had the restaurant business until one day I caught him." She shook her head. "I was able to escape, and ever since, my life has never been the same."

"But they found you," Stacy said.

Marcy nodded "Although Anton is gone, he still has a son, Vladimir."

Stacy raised her eyebrows. "The man who brought me here to your room?"

"He wants to find my daughter but when he does, he'll kill us both."

Stacy covered her face. All her dreams of going to Paris were crushed like a broken vase.

***

A couple of weeks passed and Dana had settled in her new apartment and adapted to the routine of her new job. She loved the shop, and this particular morning, arranging the display window and dressing up the mannequin in a swimsuit in time for the summer season lifted her spirits. She pasted straw hats with sunglasses on the pane and added purses as well.

"Wow," her tall, skinny and blond assistant, Courtney Wales appeared from behind. "You're good."

Her cheeks flushed as she titled her head. "Thank you."

Courtney hung swimsuits on a rack. "I'm serious." She popped her gum. "The lady who used to work here didn't care *shit* about how the shop looked. She just sat behind the counter and chatted on Facebook."

Dana shrugged. "So why didn't you manage this shop?"

Courtney swayed her head from side to side. "'Cuz this ain't my career. I want to be a model." Marching around the shop, she added. "I wanna walk down the runway and grace every fashion magazine." Then blew a bubble, and it popped.

Nodding, Dana arranged the purses.

"There's a lot of talent here in Austin, you know," she added, removing a fashion magazine from the rack.

"I have yet to explore Austin."

Courtney flipped through the pages of *Vogue* magazine and pointed to a woman posing for *Revlon* makeup. "I wanna be just like her."

Dana dropped the tray of scarves as she spotted her face on the magazine. She remembered the day of her pictorial. The hair stylist had applied too many chemicals on her hair and the makeup artist had to airbrush her look. At the end of the day, they must have taken more than a hundred photos to get the right look. Studying at the situation now, Dana didn't think she could still do that. "Um, yeah, she looks beautiful."

"Beautiful?" Courtney bent down to pick up the tray and positioned it correctly. "She's drop dead gorgeous. I can imagine what it must be like for Dana Simmons. I would trade one day of my life to be her."

Dana cursed under her breath. *No, you wouldn't.*

Courtney continued to blabber on as she perused the magazine.

She glanced at her watch. "We have five minutes before the crowd'll start blazing in."

After returning the magazine inside the rack, Courtney tidied up the shop and approached the counter. "You know you can be a model, too." She pulled out a stool and sat down, studying Dana from head to toe. "Why don't you come with me for an audition this Saturday?"

"Me?" Dana chuckled. "No thanks. Not my thing."

Courtney crossed her legs. "Why waste your good looks? I tell you, I'm grabbing the first gig that can get me to New York."

Dana spotted a customer outside and grinned, appreciating the distraction. "And here goes our day."

***

That evening, after retouching her roots, Dana filed her nails while watching TV. At this time in Bluewater Acres, she would have been tucking

Molly to sleep and reading her a bedtime story. Jake would be brushing his teeth and getting ready for bed. It had been almost six months since her life was normal since that walk she took in Central Park. Fingering her locket, she missed her parents even more.

Would Vladimir have come straight to her Manhattan apartment had she not taken a stroll along Central park that day? Why didn't he just kill her and her mother? What did he want from her? Austin may be a bustling city and she appreciated the people who came in her shop were mostly tourists and transients, but she only had to stay there because of Vladimir. Dana enjoyed the food and the friendly people, but refused to get attached. She had never felt so alone, but at least, at home, she could be herself. Dana rose and approached her closet. Brushing her fingers on her black dress, she sighed. It's a Saturday night. From her apartment, she often saw people flocking in and out of the Scarlet Lounge. Why not? Why can't she go?

In no time, she changed into her cocktail dress and put on her high heels. Dana crossed the street and entered the bar. She drew in the smoke in her lungs, strode to the empty corner table and slipped into the seat. When was the last time she got all dressed up for a night like this?

A couple at the next table flirted with each other. In the past, she used to make heads turn, but nobody seemed to be paying attention to her with her glasses and hair tied in a bow. U.S. Marshall Collins was right—a new hairstyle with a different shade could change the way you looked. Match it with glasses, and nobody would even take a second look.

Out of the corner of her eye, she spotted boisterous, tipsy women trying hard to attract the single men in the bar. The waiter brought her a martini, and she took one gulp. Music began to go full swing, and the patrons leaped to their feet to dance. Dana ordered one more drink until she told herself, she'd rather be at home in her pajamas watching TV.

***

With two women at his side, Vladimir blew out smoke from his Cuban cigar, gazing at the full moon of his Miami penthouse.

The blond escort he paid tiptoed to the balcony and removed her lingerie. "Can they see me from up here?" She giggled.

The brunette followed her and did the same thing. Then the two of them danced and touched each other as Vladimir watched.

I'm getting tired of this shit! Vladimir's cell phone vibrated. He excused himself and opened the sliding door to enter his unit. "Yep."

"They spotted her at the Scarlet Lounge in Austin." A raspy voice filtered over the line.

"Austin?" He eyed his watch. "Can you book me on the next flight?"

"Already did. Your plane leaves at six in the morning."

"Great, I owe you one," Vladimir said grabbing his keys.

***

The morning after, Dana removed the new stocks of soap and lotion, displaying them on the shelf.

"That smells so good." Courtney carried over two cups of coffee. "I got this for us."

"Oh, thank you. Very thoughtful of you."

"Guess what?" She set the cups on the counter. "I auditioned for the modeling gig, and I got a call this morning that they want me to come back for more pictorials."

"That's great news." Her eyes widened.

"I know." Courtney drummed her fingers on the counter then straightened her skirt. "It's been a lifetime dream of mine. I want to travel the world, buy all the *Chanel* purses, and hob nob with the rich and famous. I'm not getting stuck in this shop. Oops." She covered her mouth. "I didn't mean to say that."

"It's okay." Dana emptied the boxes. "We all have different dreams."

"I've been telling you all about my goals, and you've been so quiet. C'mon, share with me."

Dana didn't know what to say, so she forced a smile. "I'm going to shove these boxes in the dumpster outside."

"Oh, sure."

When Dana returned, customers flooded in all the way to closing time. Dana straightened the purses at the left back corner. Courtney counted the money from the cash register when a clean-shaven man with hair gelled to the side entered the shop, his gaze fixated on the charmed bracelets near the counter.

Courtney set the money inside the envelope and cleared her throat. "Can I help you?"

He forced a smile. "I'm looking for a gift for a friend, but I'm not sure what she would like."

"Oh, I can help you with that." Courtney tucked a strand of hair behind her ear. "Is she a girly girl or does she prefer bold colors?"

He eyed Courtney then glanced at Dana. "I'm not really sure. Maybe you both can help me out. We only went out once, but I'm really fond of her."

"Hmm, you definitely want to show her that you're interested, but don't want to come out like you're too aggressive," Courtney said. "Right, Abigail?"

Dana removed the empty hangers and set them beneath the counter. "Um, yeah, I suppose."

"Just what I needed, two women who can offer me some advice." His gaze narrowed in on Dana. "What do you have to say?"

"Well…" Dana folded her arms. "Maybe you can give her one of our scented lotions or candles. Every woman would appreciate that."

"Seems like a good idea." He nodded.

"Let me show you." Courtney led him to the aisle of lotions, but the man continued to watch Dana. Courtney opened a bottle and made him smell it. "What do you think?"

He laughed. "That smells sexy. Anything you choose would be a winner."

"All right." She giggled. "I can gift-wrap it as well for you." She brought the bottle to the counter while he trailed behind.

"That would be awesome."

"I'm Courtney." She handed him a business card. "And Abigail is the manager here."

He smiled. "Very please to meet you ladies. I'm Giovanni Amorosi. You can call me Gio for short."

"Oh, Gio." Courtney blushed as she wrapped the gift. "That's such a unique name. You must be Italian."

"My father is."

"Nice to meet you," Dana said.

"Here you go." Courtney handed him the wrapped gift. "And please don't be a stranger."

"Oh, trust me. I won't." He winked then exited the shop.

Dana shook her head.

"What?" Courtney opened her eyes wide.

"I need to teach you to be discreet."

"Oh, c'mon. Don't tell me you didn't find him cute?"

"He *is* cute, but he's twice your age."

Courtney removed her stilettos. "I'm not dating anyone my age. Twenty-something men are still boys, and the majority of them have no money. This man looks juicy and rich," she moaned. "Not to mention, he smelled good."

Dana rolled her eyes. "How do you know he's not a serial killer?"

"You're such a prude. You need to come out with me some time. I can teach you to have fun."

"That's okay. I'd rather stay at home and watch movies in my PJ's."

"You won't meet anyone that way. Don't waste your good looks, my friend. Flirt while you still have it."

"All right, all right. Well, we better make sure the cash balances so I can deposit it tomorrow."

"Yes, Mom." Courtney salutes Dana then counts the remaining bills. "There you go. It's all good."

"Thanks, my dear, see you tomorrow."

"Ciao."

Dana waves goodbye then crosses the street to head home. *Courtney's right. He is cute!*

Chapter 20

The next day, Dana tidied up the shop as Courtney smoked outside. Eager to go home, Dana heard Courtney's high heels clanking on the floor with another footsteps trailing from behind.

"Abigail, looks who's here," she said, breathless.

Dana peered from her glasses. Gio, wearing all black with matching ebony boots, smiled directly at her from the entrance.

"Gio has three tickets to see Indigo band at the Scarlet Lounge tonight, and I already said yes for us." She winked. "I told him we were available."

Dana cleared her throat, cursing underneath her breath. She gave them her heart-stopping smile and twirled her hair. "I'm sorry, but I already made plans for tonight. I wish you told me earlier."

"Oh." Courtney pouted, her cherry red lips. "How presumptuous of me to think you were available." Then facing Gio, she added, "Looks like it's just the two of us."

"Very well." Gio glanced at Dana then back at Courtney. "Perhaps we can schedule another event with Ms. Madison in advance."

"You guys have fun," Dana waved, her heart throbbing at the way Gio looked at her. She never thought she would see him again.

"Oh, we will." Courtney glimmered and clutched Gio's arm as they exited the shop.

***

Vladimir jumped out of bed and got into the shower. Courtney lay fast asleep on her stomach, her mouth curled open. He hated how aggressive these twenty-year-old women were, so eager like a puppy dog waiting to be pet. The first time he saw Dana, he expected to see a woman with silicone lips and Botox, but everything about her spelled the opposite. She had milk skin, and her eyes glimmered behind her glasses. Her beauty possessed simplicity combined with elegance. She didn't need make-up and looked much prettier in person. He couldn't help but notice how gracious and refined her demeanor exuded.

The hot water poured on his body as he lathered soap all over. Why did he feel this way? What happened to his angry motives. Vladimir reminded himself not to get carried away. After toweling off, he opened the drawer and cocked his gun. *I'm here for one mission.*

***

Dana had just finished helping a customer when Courtney arrived late that morning with her hair disheveled and no makeup on.

"Good morning. I thought you weren't coming."

Courtney yawned. "Sorry, late night."

"I presumed." Dana grinned.

Courtney plopped her bag behind the counter. "My body is all sore."

"You what?" She shook her head. "How many times do I have to tell you not to have sex on your first date?"

"Yes, Mom." She rolled her eyes. "You should have been a nun."

Dana folded her arms. "You need people to respect you, Courtney. What challenge will the guy have if you're so easy?"

Courtney sat at the counter. She blew a bubble and popped it. "I don't think he's one of those guys who will take me for a ride. He made me speak to his cousin who said he knows of an agent in New York that can help me with my career."

"And you believe him?"

Before Courtney could answer, Gio walked in with two cups of lattes. "Good morning, ladies." He pressed his lips against Courtney, who embraced him tight.

"You missed me already?" Eyeing Dana, she took the cups from him and set them on the countertop.

Smiling at Dana, he faced Courtney. "I came to deliver the good news. If it's okay with Ms. Madison, I've booked you on a flight tomorrow morning for New York." He removed a ticket from his pocket. "You are all set to meet with Rob Hanson the famous agent who, mind you, is a photographer as well."

Courtney planted kisses on Gio. "You're my angel. I knew from the minute you walked in the shop that day."

Rob? Courtney will be meeting Rob? She fiddled with the pen and pretended to scribble a number. How she wished she could send a note to Rob that she was alive and safe.

"Did you hear that Abigail?" She giggled. "Is it okay if I leave?"

Dana took a deep breath, turned around and straightened her shoulders. "That's fabulous. This has been your ultimate dream." She squeezed Courtney's arms. "You can't possibly give up on this opportunity." Then towards Gio, she added, "Thank you for doing this for her. You don't know how much it means to Courtney."

He flashed her a dreamy look. "No sweat."

"Thanks, honey." Courtney opened the envelope. "And you bought me a business class ticket?" She clapped her hands in delight then embraced him. "You totally spoil me."

Two customers walked in, and Gio cleared his throat. "Won't stay long. Just wanted to share the good news."

Dana waved goodbye then attended to the clients while Courtney escorted Gio outside. *Who is this man and why is he doing this for Courtney?*

***

That was the only confirmation Vladimir needed—the look on Abigail Madison's face. She could no longer hide her disguise. *Dana Simmons* While Courtney spent time in New York, he could get cozy with Dana and get to know the real her. He had to wait till she was vulnerable and for her to open up to him.

156

Vladimir called Constantine. "It's really her. I'm most certain it is."

"What are you going to do?"

"I'll keep you posted. I trust you'll be responsible while I'm away."

Laughter exploded. "I should be asking you the same question. I hope you don't do anything stupid."

Lighting a cigarette, Vladimir inhaled. "You know I won't. Just watch, I'll have her falling for me in no time."

***

Rob continued to keep himself busy with work to avoid thinking of Dana. He still couldn't believe Dana was in Europe. Her contract with most products was ending in six months, and as her agent, he would either have to renew them or find new product endorsements for her.

He opened his mailbox at the lobby of his apartment building and ripped the only envelope open. Pulling out three headshots, he read the note.

This is the lady I was telling you about, Courtney Wales. She'll be at your studio tomorrow at three pm.

"Not bad at all," he mumbled. He was used to getting referrals from friends of friends. Everyone wanted to be a model.

***

Dana was closing the shop when Gio approached.

"You scared me." She froze. *Why is he here?*

"I'm sorry. I wanted to check if you were okay." He blushed. "I mean, I'm to blame for leaving you without an assistant."

Dana drew in a breath. *Why does he have to be so charming?* "You were doing her a favor." She buried the keys inside her purse.

"How about I do *you* a favor as well?"

She took a step forward. "Thanks, but don't think I need anything for now."

"You'll surely need help to watch the store." He pointed to the "We're hiring" sign in the window.

"It's all right." Dana paused, gathering her thoughts. *How do I dismiss him?* "It will only be for a few days."

He chuckled. "I don't think so."

She took an exasperated breath.

"Knowing Courtney, she'll come back to offer her resignation. I mean, look at her. She's beautiful, and I'm sure the agent would love her."

"And how well do you know this agent?" She paused. *Maybe she shouldn't have said that.*

He shrugged. "Oh, me? I don't know him. He happens to know the coworker of a friend. You know, that type of thing."

"Right."

"So what do you say? I temp for you while she's gone?"

"You?" She raised her eyebrows.

"Sure. Never worked with a man before?"

She pursed her lips. "Well, I need to talk to the owner and see what I can do, but this job doesn't seem like your type of thing"

Pulling out his wallet, Gio gave her his business card. "Call me I'm flexible." And he was gone like smoke.

Dana stared at the business card. *Giovanni Amorosi Importer/Trader. Hmmm...Why would he want to work here?*

Chapter 21

Rob dimmed the lighting in his studio as a tall, blond slender woman marched in.

The woman set her purse in the counter. "Are you Rob Hanson?"

He extended his hand. "You must be Courtney."

"Pleasure to meet you." She gave him a tight grip, her palm cold and clammy.

Grabbing his camera, he circled around the studio. "I'd like to take some shots of you."

"Sure." She straightened her skirt and fixed her salmon silk scarf.

Rob positioned a chair in the center of the floor. "Let's do some of you sitting down."

Courtney plopped herself on the chair while Rob did some test shots from each angle.

"Have you modeled before?"

"I did some gigs in Austin, but they were small ones."

Rob peered into the lens. "I'd like you to pull your hair back in a ponytail."

She followed his instructions and titled her head.

"Perfect, love it. Now, let's get one of you standing up and leaning your body against the wall."

Rising from her seat, Courtney approached the corner and rested her weight on the wall.

Rob studied her while he snapped photos. "I love that you have a touch of apricot. It lightens up your face."

"Really?" A smile spread on her lips. "You don't know how many outfits I tried on this morning."

He grinned, opening a folder that contained her resume. "Is this your usual weight? Or did you lose weight before coming here?"

"I'm a hundred and twenty pounds, but before my period, I can go to one twenty five. Will that be a problem?"

Rob laid the camera on the chair and tested the lighting. "As a photographer, I prefer curvier women, but as an agent, I'm strict and tough." He looked at her straight in the eye. "I'm not going to sugar it for you. Modeling is a cruel industry, and you gotta have thick skin to survive."

Courtney pressed her lips together.

"You need to lose at least five to seven pounds. You can't have the roots of your hair revealing a different shade from the rest, and I don't mean to be rude, but please throw out your gum."

"Does that mean I don't have a chance?" She spit out her gum into a Kleenex she pulled from her purse and tossed it inside the garbage can.

Rob burst into laughter. "Of course you do. You're amazingly beautiful. You have the height and body. You're young and have a vibrant personality. I wanted to check if you can handle the critic because people can be downright mean in this industry. And I totally want to represent you. For now, it will be easier for me to get you to do print, like magazines, over runway shows. Are you okay with that?"

She leaped to her feet and gave Rob a tight embrace. "Oh my gosh, of course. And I will lose those pounds and dye my roots once I leave your studio."

"Great. Let's take more shots so I can send this to my contacts. They're looking for fresh new faces, and I believe you'd be a great fit."

"Wow, Gio was right. He promised you'd take care of me."

Turning off the lights, Rob packed his cameras. "Let me prepare the contract."

After signing the contract, Rob realized how he missed Dana. Projects were lining up and how he wished he could give them to Dana.

***

Vladimir read the text on his phone, and that was all he needed. *Courtney signed contract. Turn on your computer.*

A warm smile spread on his lips.

Taking a stroll, he crossed the street and dashed inside his motel which was two blocks away from Dana's house.

He grabbed his laptop and turned it on, rubbing his hands as he studied the view of Rob's loft. Punching a text on his phone, he said, *Well done.*

***

A couple of weeks had passed since Courtney left, and whether Dana liked it or not, Gio had been right. Rob had booked Courtney a contract with a clothing line, and even as a runway model. She deserved it, but now Dana was left with Gio to manage the store.

Gio worked harder than Courtney. He arrived earlier than usual, never eyed the clock, greeted customers, provided them the utmost care, and always brought her tea. He was submissive and accommodating at all times.

As they did the final inventory that afternoon, Gio said, "I suggest that we have a one-day sale tomorrow. Slash everything to fifty percent."

Working on a spreadsheet sales forecast, Dana glanced at him. "I don't know if the owner will agree."

"You can tell her you want to get rid of the old stock and increase sales. It's just one day."

"You're right." She chewed on the tip of her pen. "Why didn't I think of that?"

"Well, that's why you need me here."

They shared a laugh.

"That's the first time I've ever heard you laugh."

She covered her mouth.

"Seriously, you should laugh more often."

He was damn right. When was the last time she laughed?

"Hey, how about I take you to dinner tonight?"

"Dinner?"

"Yeah, you need to eat. Nothing fancy." He gestured. "I heard there's a nice Japanese restaurant across the street. What do you say we go try it."

Dana took a long time to answer. *I can't be alone all the time.* She missed Rob back home, and Jake, Molly and Sarah back in Bluewater Acres, and she felt bad that she didn't even go out to dinner with Courtney. Gio looked like a nice and harmless guy, and what was wrong with having dinner? "I don't know. I still have to put tags on the new stock."

"Okay, but you gotta eat. How about I bring you dinner instead?"

Before she could say anything, Gio fled to the door.

Persistent. She couldn't deny she enjoyed the attention he gave her.

***

Rob rolled his suitcase inside his loft and flung his keys on the counter. Exhausted from his morning photo shoot, he sank onto his couch and turned on his laptop. He opened his drawer and removed the contents from an envelope–checks made to Dana Simmons. How long would it take until these checks became stale? Six months? Less? He eyed the calendar on his desk and marked September "the month I find Dana."

His phone disturbed his thoughts. He answered, "Yeah?"

"Did you meet the woman I told you about?" a faint, high-pitched voice asked.

"Sandy? Yes, I did." He cleared his throat. "I know she's a friend of your cousin, and I owe you a huge favor, but just to be frank, she needs to build her class."

Laughter erupted over the phone. "I know what you mean. She has a few rough edges, but hey, I'm sure Courtney will step up to the plate."

Rob grinned. "You'll be thrilled to note that she signed her first contract with a new clothing brand." He turned on his laptop and clicked on Courtney's photos.

"That's awesome. I owe you one, buddy."

"No problem. I appreciate the referrals."

"You take care, my friend," she added.

The phone clicked as he continued to browse the photos. His cursor landed on the pictures he took of Michael Downey's house. He had looked at them several times since his visit, but never found anything and the agents never noticed suspicious activity.

Rob decided to look at it again, and this time something caught his eye. He zoomed to get a closer look.

"Holy shit!" Rob blinked. "This can't be."

Right before Rob's eyes was a reflection of Michael Downey's PC, and on the screen were four young women exposing their bodies. *Why didn't I look for this earlier?*

Then he remembered the mirror that was hung on the wall of Michael Downey's living room. "Oh my God." He zoomed it, and his jaw dropped. *Stacy Kestav.*

***

Weeks had passed and Stacy and Marcy had bonded while they were in captive.

"How long do you think they'll keep us here?" Stacy asked that morning.

Marcy squeezed her hand. "Do you believe in hope?"

"I'd like to."

"Every day, I tell myself that I'm closer to seeing my daughter again. I will never stop thinking of her beautiful smile. I know we will be together again."

Tears spilled down Stacy's cheeks. "I miss my sister and my mom." Her face grew grim. "But I will never forgive my father for what he did. I will see that he rots in jail."

Marcy embraced her. "Hang onto your hope. You have a whole life ahead of you."

***

Rob leaned against Stanley's desk while his lawyer browsed the photos in his camera. "That's Stacy Kestav."

Stanley pursed his lips. "The picture is not that clear. How can you tell it's her?"

Rob zoomed the next photo, which showed a sunflower tattoo on the lady's belly button. "I remember her tattoo."

Swinging his chair, Stanley rose from his seat and opened the refrigerator in the corner. He grabbed two cans of Coke and tossed one to Rob. "Did you call the FBI agents already?"

"Not yet. I wanted to check with you first. This sure is Goddamn proof that he has something to do with Stacy Kestav's case."

"You're putting yourself at risk."

"I didn't come here for your approval." Rob circled around the desk and plopped himself on the chair. "I came here to tell you that I will need your help."

Stanley raised his eyebrows. "I have to admit that you're just like your father. You don't take no for an answer."

Rob folded his arms.

"You know very well that if there's a case, we can't present this as evidence since you were inside private property."

"I didn't break in his house. I was invited in."

Stanly exhaled an exasperated breath. "And you were using an alias."

"Who gives a fuck. The evidence is there. Stacy could still be alive."

"You don't even know if that's an old photo."

"You're not making this any easier for me." Disgusted, Rob headed for the door and took one last look at Stanley. "If you don't want to help me, then I might as well do this on my own. I don't wait for things to happen, I make things happen."

Chapter 22

On the phone, Vladimir waited for his order outside the restaurant.

"Did you check your computer today?" Constantine asked.

"I'm not home. What's up?"

"What's the matter with you? You're losing your guard and not covering your tracks."

"What do you mean?" Vladimir looked behind to see if anybody was following him. No one was there.

"I hacked into Rob Hanson's computer. You'd be interested to know that your pretend Seattle realtor happens to be the same photographer and agent that signed up Courtney for her modeling career. But after downloading her photos, he happened to notice the pictures he took at your house."

"He took photos of my house?"

"Yeah, and thanks to your feng shui guru who told you to hang a mirror on the wall—"

"Wait, wait. What do you mean?" He kicked a stone on the sidewalk.

"It caught the reflection of your laptop where you had naked photos of Stacy Kestav."

"Holy sh—" He covered his mouth, eyeing the patrons who entered the restaurant.

"I'm texting you the photo now."

Vladimir checked the picture. His heart sank like a deflated balloon.

"I'm taking care of it."

Vladimir didn't say a word.

"I don't know what the fuck is wrong with you, Vladimir. You're weak, and your emotions are clouding your vision."

"Look, I'm this close to getting her to open up to me."

"And what are you going to do after that?"

"Slow down, boy. The best way to treat your enemies is to make them your friend. Once you have their trust, you use your power against their vulnerability."

"I admire your patience," Constantine said. "While you're doing your rendezvous, you need to know that the gang and I have been doing all your work."

"And you know how much I appreciate you for that."

"You need to get your ass back here soon. No more careless mistakes."

"I will." He watched the stream of people coming down from the train.

The waiter walked out of the restaurant and interrupted his conversation. "Here's your order."

"Look, I gotta go. Talk soon." *Fuck! How could I be so careless?*

***

After sharpening her chopsticks, Dana plunged the avocado roll inside her mouth. She wiped her lips with a napkin and moaned. "This is so delicious."

"I told you you needed to eat."

Scribbling on her pad, Dana wrote: *Reminder: Abigail needs to eat.*

He grinned, and moved the soy sauce closer to her. "I wasn't sure if you were allergic to anything or a if you're a vegetarian so I got a mixture of everything."

She aimed for the cha-ya roll, she said, "This is a feast. Thank you."

"So…" He sipped his sake. "I don't think I asked you, but how long have you managed the shop?"

"Just recently." She chewed hoping he wouldn't ask where she grew up but he did.

"Are you a Texas native?"

She took a deep breath, but kept her gaze glued on her meal. "Nope. Originally from Georgia and moved here five years ago."

"Hmm." he pressed his lips together. "You don't seem to have a Southern accent."

"You think so," she practiced her drawl wondering why U.S. Marshall Collins had thought of Georgia.

"Now that's better. What did you do before managing this shop?"

"Well…" She paused, realizing that inventing stories was all she did for the past months. "Waitressing, selling cars, you name it."

"Really? And what made you choose this job?"

He seemed to be asking too many questions. She cleaned up the last sushi on her plate. "It's not rocket science." Dana giggled. "It's fun. I don't know if I'll be here for a long time, but I think it would probably be nice to own my own shop someday."

"Interesting." He nodded.

After a moment, Dana realized that *was* what she wanted. Managing this shop allowed her to use her fashion sense to arrange the store the way she wanted it to be. She kept the show window fresh and hip every week. Sales had doubled since she started, and she liked that she had the freedom to choose what to buy from vendors. For the first time in months, she learned something about herself, and whether she was Dana Simmons, Lucy Mitchell, or Abigail Madison, this was something she wanted.

"You're very good at what you do," he added.

"Oh, thank you." She felt herself blush. "But enough of about me. Tell me about yourself. What exactly do you import?"

"Anything and everything."

"Quite vague, huh?" *Why is he so mysterious?*

He leaned forward to reach for the salmon sashimi.

Dana and Gio spent the rest of the evening enjoying the meal and chatting.

After Dana locked the shop from outside, Gio took her hand. "Let me take you home."

"No need." She gently pulled away. "I live close by."

"I don't bite," he joked. "A lady like you shouldn't be walking alone late at night."

"It's all right." She waved away his concern. "I'll be fine."

"Okay, if you insist."

"See you tomorrow."

He reached out to kiss her on the cheek, but as she moved her head, the kiss landed on her lips.

She pulled away, heart beating fast and never expecting a kiss so abrupt.

"Be safe," he said.

***

Dana nuzzled against the pillow, feeling the softness of the satin sheets. Gio's kiss caught her off guard and gave her butterflies in her stomach. She had thought about Jake, but Gio seemed more exciting, spontaneous but she wondered if he still liked Courtney. When was the last time someone ever kissed her on the lips? Not that she could get too close.

Turning on her lamp, Dana opened her night table drawer and plucked out her calendar. There was one goal she needed to fulfill before she could open her own shop and fall in love. Summer was blazing hot and in full swing. She flipped the pages to August and scribbled: *The month I kill Vladimir.*

Chapter 23

A cold gust of wind brushed upon Rob's back as he typed on his laptop. Rising from his seat, he approached the front door and noticed it was ajar. Checking inside, he marched back to his desk. *Did someone break in? I know I locked the door.*

Peering to the window, nobody seemed to be in sight. He circled back to his desk.

Strong hands covered his face. Gasping for air, Rob tried to scream. He elbowed the person and tried to reach for something to pull but everything went blank.

***

Leaning on his pillow, Vladimir watched the scene as Constantine and four members of the mob invaded Rob's house, stealing his laptop and camera. Moments after, they dumped the brutally stabbed body of Stacy Kestav's body on the couch beside Rob who remained unconscious.

He covered his face as his throat constricted. There was no way he could continue this life. How could he have lived this life—his father's life? He needed an escape plan.

***

"I swear to God I had nothing to do with this," Rob cried as a policeman handcuffed him.

"You're under arrest. You have the right to remain silent, a right to an attorney. If you don't have one, the court can appoint one for—"

"They set me up. I had been working on my laptop. Somebody came from behind and covered my mouth, the next thing I know, I woke up with Stacy's dead body beside me."

He glanced around frantically. The CSI team surveyed his loft, gathering the bloody knife and taking pictures of the scene.

The cop shook his head. "Try explaining that to the jury."

"There was no sign of a break in," another cop added.

"I am no damn criminal," Rob yelled while they dragged him to the car. "I need to talk to FBI Agent Wayne. Please get him on the phone." *If Stacy's dead, what if Dana's next.*

***

FBI Agents Wayne and Raymond stood at the back as the crowd gathered for the burial of Stacy Kestav.

"Look at Mr. Kestav." Felicia nudged him. "He doesn't seem to have any emotion while his wife and daughter can't stop crying."

Kerry eyed the father. "I'm sure he's grieving inside."

"I don't know about you, but I don't trust him."

"You think he planted Stacy's body at Rob's house?" Kerry asked.

"Nothing would surprise me anymore," Felicia said.

***

Rob banged his hand on the wall. All he saw were the four corners of his enclosed jail cell with a urinal. "Get me out of here." The dim lights and stillness scared the wits out of him. Racing thoughts of the last image he saw of Stacy in his studio haunted him. *Who would do such a thing?*

The lights turned on and the guards dragged him out. "You have a visitor."

They led him to the lounge where the familiar sound of squeaky pair of shoes approached him. Rob fixed his gaze on his lawyer.

"Rob, I'm here."

"Right." Rob leaned one foot to the wall. "They set me up, Stanley."

"I'm going to get you out of here in no time."

"Why don't you get me out now?"

"I can't. As it is you're the main suspect. Bail is one million."

"Where is Agent Wayne? Why haven't they called him?" Rob's heart sank. "I never did this. You need to investigate Stacy's family again. Something's fishy. You have to show the cops the photos I showed you."

Stanley folded his arms. "I'm afraid your laptop and camera aren't there."

"Are you freaking kidding me?" Rob shrieked. "They set me up. You know that."

"Trust me, I'm going to dig some dirt."

"I know, I know, but you know how these cops are. They'll try to find every motive they can get to pin on me. The press has to be out there sensationalizing the scandal."

Rob didn't say a word.

"You stay put here. You gotta trust me on this."

Rob couldn't believe the series of events. All he ever wanted was to find Dana and now this?

***

After applying cold cream to her face, Dana tied her hair up and removed the cell phone from her emergency backpack U.S. Marshall Collins gave her. Each time U.S. Marshall Collins checked on Dana, he reminded her not to get close to anyone and to alert him for any suspicious activity. Today, she decided to call him.

"Hello, Abigail."

"It's Dana."

"You know that Abigail is—"

"Right, right. Listen, I've just had an epiphany."

"Epiphany?"

"Yeah." She slipped into her pajamas. "I want to open my own shop."

"You already manage one."

"It's not the same. I want my own where I can develop my own line."

"So you want to be an entrepreneur."

Dana frowned. "Am I not allowed to have dreams?"

"We all have *dreams*, Abigail, but for now, you don't want to attract too much attention."

Sighing, Dana added, "What is the big deal? I'll be doing the exact same thing, except it's mine. I don't even have to say I own the shop."

Silence crossed between them.

"Look, I'm sorry that I even asked." She hung up and paced around the room. *Why do I have to listen to the Feds?*

The phone rang, but Dana tossed it back in her backpack and left it on her bed.

She changed out of her pajamas, slipped into a faded pair of jeans and a gray tee, and stormed out of her house. After crossing the street, she walked two blocks before reaching Cupcakes Corner, a place where they sold vegan cupcakes. She truly needed a chocolate fix.

After buying cupcakes, she sat in a booth, devouring the icing.

After taking a generous bite, she spotted Gio paying the cashier. "Gio."

He didn't hear her the first time, so she waved to him.

"Hey." He raised his eyebrows as he approached her. "You're craving too, huh?"

"Yeah, come join me."

"Oh." He glanced at his watch. "I was going to eat it a home but…"

"Sorry. You can go." She gestured her hands in the air.

"I can watch the game later." He took a seat beside her.

"Thanks, Gio. You're a great friend."

They ate their cupcakes in silence.

"Why so blue?" He stroked her cheek.

Her heart fluttered as he stared at her. "Do you think that you have everything figured out?"

"What do you mean?" He eyed her intently.

"You know… life." She sighed wishing she could just open up to him about what she'd been through.

He clutched her hand. "Let's get out of here."

***

Dana had not ridden in someone's car for a long time, but as the wind swept her hair away, all she wanted was to run away with Gio and take care of him even if a part of her feared he was a womanizer. Tonight, she wanted to forget everything—forget she was Abigail Madison or Dana Simmons. Tonight, she would focus on being a woman with no past and no future, just the present.

"Where are you taking me?"

"Just wait." He parked his Bentley near the curb.

She enjoyed gazing at him, how classy he dressed, how he ate, and most of all, how he treated a woman. "Do you keep in touch with Courtney?"

Grinning, he stepped out of the car, walked around to her side, and opened her door. "Abigail, I want you to know that there is nothing going on between me and Courtney. She's very young and I—"

"I'm sorry I asked."

"Hey." He massaged her shoulders. "Tonight, we don't have to think about Courtney or work. Tonight, we get to have fun."

"You're right." She marched beside him.

"Close your eyes." He held her hand.

Taking a deep breath, she gripped his hand and closed her eyes. U.S. Marshall Collins warned her to trust nobody, but she was tired of taking care of herself. If only she could tell someone about her secret. She missed having a friend she could talk to.

"It will only be a moment," he said as he guided her.

Using her other senses, she heard the clinking of high heels against what sounded like marble floors. She smelled fresh lavender scent.

"We're almost there."

This time, Dana heard the sound of an elevator and people chattering. It seemed like an eternity, but Gio never let go of her hand. For once she felt safe.

Finally, the elevator opened and Gio led her out. She heard him fiddling with his keys and opening a door. They strode inside, and this time, he held her arms positioning her from behind.

"Okay, you can open your eyes now."

Slowly, Dana opened her eyes and dropped her jaw as she stood in the balcony overlooking the harbor and city of Austin. She gazed at the boats anchored in the water and surveyed the lights around the area. Stars dazzled in the sky and left footprints in her heart.

"What do you think?"

She turned to see as he now carried two wine glasses and champagne. "Is this where you live?"

After pouring champagne, he clinked her glass with his. "When I'm in Austin."

Taking a sip, Dana faced the view. "How long will you be in Austin?"

He joined her. "As long as you need me, I'm here."

"But what if I don't need you?" she hinted with a grin.

He leaned close to her and pressed his lips against hers. "Are you sure you don't?"

Closing her eyes, she opened her mouth as he gently caressed her tongue. He tasted like champagne laced with chocolate cupcake. He ran his fingers through her hair, and she found herself drowning in lust.

She pulled away, breathless, tucking a strand of her hair behind her ears. "We shouldn't."

He nodded, taking a step back. "I'm sorry."

"No." She rubbed her face, her hand was wet. "It's been a long time for me."

He rested his hands on hers. "I understand. I'm a very patient man."

She dried her tears. *Why did life have to be so complicated?*

"Whenever I try to figure out life, I stay up here. I can stare at the view for hours. It's a reminder that there's something bigger than whatever we are facing now."

Dana gazed at him then affixed her eyes on the stars above. "Do you ever wish you lived a different life from what you have now?"

"That's one question I ask myself, yet I can't seem to answer that."

"Do you believe you can change your fate?"

He took a deep breath. "I know it sounds cliché, but I believe you can do anything you want to do if you put your heart into it."

Dana looked at him straight in the eye and kissed him. She wanted him, needed him and for now she didn't care about tomorrow.

Chapter 24

Slipping her key inside the door, Dana unlocked the bolt and carried her sandals inside. She rested her purse on the counter and went to the kitchen to get water. She was still bedazzled over the lovemaking she and Gio shared that evening. After taking a huge gulp of water, she headed to the living room.

She turned on the lights and screamed.

U.S. Marshall Collins sat on her couch.

"You scared me."

He folded his arms. "You don't answer your phone or return my calls."

"Gosh, can't I even have time to myself?"

"You sounded upset yesterday about wanting to open your own shop. If I allowed you to do that, you'd be establishing roots which will be difficult to let go in case you need to run away."

"How long is this going to take? Have you caught them yet?" She snarled.

"You know the answer to that question."

"My modeling contracts are going to expire before the year ends," she said.

"Which means we have to do a memorial for you.

"What?"

"Oh, you heard me. We have to fake your death. I tried to make this easy for you, but I don't think you realize how serious this matter is."

"Easy," she lashed out. "You've never been stripped out your identity, dragged from place to place, unable to get close to anyone. I miss being able to have a friend where I can just laugh and share a secret. I want to be able to talk about who I am and what I dream of. I wish I could express myself to my full potential. I don't want to settle for average."

"I'm sorry."

"Why do I have to listen to you? What difference does it make to live like this when I've lost my family and myself? What more do I have to live for?"

She immediately thought of Gio and how special he made her feel. How she enjoyed watching him sleep peacefully before she tiptoed outside his unit. How she took one last look at the view of the city, and how she wanted to get lost from everything.

She'd tell Gio her secret soon, and maybe he can help her fulfill her goal—to kill Vladimir, locate the Russian mob, and rescue her mother. She needed Gio to help her. She couldn't count on the Feds. But she also couldn't possibly do it alone.

So, she gave U.S. Marshall Collins her heart-stopping smile. "Do you want me to write my obituary?"

***

Gio slipped into his robe and grabbed his phone. After punching in a number, he keyed in a text. *It worked. She trusts me now.*

His phone beeped. *Good. How long?*

Patience, my cowboy.

***

Dana took a gulp of her green tea as Gio entered the shop with a dozen pink roses.

"You're early." His eyes lit up when he set the vase on the counter.

"Aw, they're beautiful. Thank you."

He gave her a gentle kiss on the lips. "You left without saying goodbye."

Opening the cash register, she pulled out the stack of bills and divided them into twenties, tens and fives. "You slept like a baby."

A grin played on his lips. "Come away with me this weekend."

She shrugged wishing she could go. "You know I can't leave the store."

"What if I tell you that I can let you leave the shop?"

Shutting the cash register, she pointed out, "And I know you won't take no for an answer."

"Can't help it."

Bending down, she said, "I'm afraid I can't do this Gio. You hardly know me and you don't—"

"No need to explain." He gestured with his hands and winked. "I perfectly understand. But just so you know, the invitation is always open. It doesn't have to be this weekend."

Dana pursed her lips. "I love your persistence."

"Persistence…" He pointed up. "Is the key to success. And here comes a customer." He approached the door and welcomed a brunette inside. "Good morning, how can I help a beautiful lady like you?"

The woman blushed. "Thank you, I'm looking for a scarf."

"A scarf?" Gio led her to the aisle and fondled the array of scarves. He picked an emerald one. "To you, this may seem like an ordinary scarf." He put it around her neck. "But look at how it compliments your green eyes."

The lady faced the mirror and beamed. "Wow."

He plucked a pair of silver dangling earrings from a nearby table. "Add this and you'll dazzle your date."

Dana covered her mouth, trying to control her laughter as the lady applied the earrings and admired herself in the mirror.

"So?" He raised his eyebrows.

"You're right," the lady said, facing him. "You're good." Turning to Dana, she added, "Can I hire him to be my fashion consultant?"

Dana giggled. "Sure, but he's worth a fortune."

The lady brought the scarf and earrings to the counter. "I can imagine." She handed Dana her credit card.

Dana rang up the items and swiped her card. She put the items in their respective boxes.

"Wow. I love the packaging. This is such a fancy shop. Do you own it?"

Dana looked away. "I just manage it."

"She doesn't just manage the shop," Gio said with conviction. "She gets to choose the products herself. She has a good eye for quality."

The woman took the paper bag. "With that keen eye, you might consider owning your own business."

Dana smiled. "I'll keep that in mind."

"Have a nice day," Gio added.

The lady waved goodbye. A stream of customers flood in and kept Dana and Gio busy till mid-afternoon.

"I'm starving. What are you in the mood for?" Gio asked while tidying the shop.

Dana folded the beach towels. "You've been such a gentleman. Let me buy you lunch for a change."

"Let's order delivery. I'm craving a nasty patty." He cackled.

"Sure, nasty patty it is."

"Oh, and that cafe also makes vegan burgers."

"Nice." Dana pressed her lips.

"You are vegan, right?"

Dana marched to the aisle behind him. "Yeah, sort of."

He followed her. "You also don't do a good job evading questions."

Dana froze. *Am I that obvious?*

He gazed at her. "What is bothering you, Abigail?"

She shook her head, tears trickling down her cheeks.

"I'm here for you." He dried her tears. "Why do I get this feeling that you're holding back?"

"What do you mean?" She walked away, trying to calm her nerves. All she wanted to do was tell him everything. Should she?

"You're not using your full potential." Gio spun her around. "You're beautiful, decent, talented and you were made to shine." Pulling her towards him, he kissed her.

Again, she got lost in his kisses and found herself caressing his hair. Gio lifted her and reached for her breast as he planted soft kisses on her neck. She unbuttoned his shirt and continued to kiss him. Oblivious to her surroundings, she laid her hands on his behind, pulling him against her.

A woman cleared her throat. "What's the meaning of all this?"

Dana and Gio let go of each other.

"Cara, I can explain this," Dana said, straightening her skirt. *Oh no!*

The woman stalked toward them, her three-inch heels clacking. "What's there to explain? You're supposed to be managing the shop and not playing pokey with your assistant. Did you forget our end of the month meeting?"

"I'm sorry." Dana tied her hair in a ponytail. "This won't happen again."

Cara circled around them. "How do I know you don't do this every day?"

"If I may say, you're not being supportive," Gio coughed. "She's an incredible manager who works ten hours a day six days a week. She hardly eats. She chooses the best products, and sales are better than the other shops in this area. If you want to blame someone, *blame* me." He laid his hand on his chest. "I kissed her. I told her that she was worth more than all of this. I care so much about her that I would want to make you an offer." He folded his arms "I would like to buy this shop for her."

Cara eyed him from head to toe. "You're quite a gentleman, but what makes you think this shop is for sale?"

He straightened his shoulders. "Name your price, and I'll double it."

Cara glanced at Dana and back at Gio as a customer walked in. "Get back to work."

Dana didn't, couldn't say a word.

***

In Gio's bedroom that night, Dana reached for his hand. "I don't know how to thank you for what you did today."

He brought her hand to his lips. "It's nothing."

She traced her finger on his jaw. "Nobody has ever stood up for me like that."

"I meant what I said. I could buy that shop for you."

She leaned on his chest. "How do you do know me so well?"

Taking a deep breath, he said, "I was born to love you."

She fingered her locket and set it on the night table allowing the words to sink in. She didn't just want to be loved, she needed to be loved. Just looking at Gio reminded her of how her father used to take care of her mother. *Home.* "I love you, Gio." She closed her eyes.

***

188

Agent Wayne tidied his desk and grabbed his jacket, ready to leave for the night, when the phone rang.

Sighing, he picked it up. "Agent Wayne here."

"Agent Wayne," a girl's voice cried. "I need to talk to you. This is Natasha."

"Natasha Kestav? Are you okay?"

"No, I'm not." She was weeping, which made her words hard to understand.. "My father, OMG, he's such a pig. He's disgusting! You need to come here right now. He doesn't know that I know."

"I'm on my way, Natasha. You have to be discreet and pretend you don't know anything."

"Please hurry."

Kerry took a deep breath. This case seemed to be leading them to more clues and he intended to get to the bottom of it all.

***

After discussing with Natasha Kestav, FBI Agents Kerry and Felicia and their team presented the warrant of arrest at Stacy Kestav's house.

Mr. Kestav held the door ajar, exposing his arm with a dragoon tattoo. "What do you guys want?"

Kerry kicked the door and pushed him towards the wall. "You're under arrest for the murder of your daughter, Stacy Kestav. You−"

"I didn't murder my daughter." He struggled with his arms, trying to get loose.

Mrs. Kestav came out of another room, hair disheveled, eyes wide open. "What's the meaning of all this?"

Natasha popped in from her room. "I called them, Mom." Her eyes guarded.

"What?" Mrs. Kestav said. "How could you do such a thing, Natasha?"

She led the team to the basement. They dragged Mr. Kestav downstairs, his wife trailing behind them. The team searched the basement and found pornography videos and monitors.

"Did you do this?" Mrs. Kestav eyed her husband. "Is this what you do when you tell me you're working late?" She slapped his face.

Natasha hugged her mother from behind. "Mom, you didn't know. He's the one who killed Stacy. There's blood down there." She pointed to the floor.

Putting on his gloves, Kerry reached underneath the desk and removed a bloody butcher knife and handed it to an officer. "I'm sure it will match Stacy's DNA. You need to tell us now who is behind this. I'm sure you work for somebody."

Mrs. Kestav shouted at her husband in Russian while Mr. Kestav didn't say a word.

Felicia approached. "You see, Mr. Kestav, one of your victims described your tattoo, and if I'm not mistaken, she called you Skully."

He wiggled his arms and his eyes were wide open, but the officers pressed their hands on him.

"Your heart rate must have jumped when I said that. You need to tell us where Marcy Simmons is," Felicia added.

Mr. Kestav spat at them as they pulled him out of his house.

Kerry turned to Felicia. "We need to find Marcy Simmons."

Chapter 25

Vladimir stopped near a ditch to catch his breath. The morning run was exhilarating and helped clear his head. No matter how hard he planned to hurt Dana, he couldn't. He was quite smitten by the supermodel and never felt this way with anyone. Vladimir passed by the ideal location where he planned to buy a property. His dream now would be to build a low-rise building that would include a gift shop for Dana. Austin's charming city won his heart, and he was ready to have a new life, but there were matters he needed to fix.

Sweat poured down his back and beads of moisture heated up on his face. He pulled out his pedometer, analyzing the steps he took.

His cell phone rang. He sighed as Constantine's number flashed on the screen. "What's up?"

"Time is ticking."

"Don't pressure me." He bent down to stretch his knees.

"They're coming for us, and you're so occupied with this woman you're wasting—"

"Constantine, you don't know what it's like to have a father constantly at your back, telling you you're not good enough. He never paid attention to me or Mom. All he cared about was that stupid bitch, Marcy, and when she left, he neglected us. I hate him for what he did to me and Mom." He squared his jaw.

"I hear you. Do what you have to do, then get your ass back here."

"I don't know." Vladimir drew in a breath, watching as other joggers passed through the trail. "Although I hated Dad, all I ever wanted was for him to love me and be proud of me."

"I'm sure he's *proud* of you."

Vladimir shook his head. "But look at me. Look at *us*. We're exactly like our dads. We joined the mob," he mumbled. "Don't you ever wonder what could have been out there for us?"

"Watch what you're saying. Are you listening to yourself?" Constantine raised his voice. "Your judgment is clouded because of this woman. How the hell can you question what we're doing when we have the perfect lifestyle? We have houses all over. We can travel when we want to. The booze, the women... Are you crazy?"

"Maybe I can just sell my shares."

"Vladimir, are you out of your mind? You've forgotten how your father built this business and you—"

"I'm not destroying the business. I'm thinking of selling my shares. That way, you can handle it and I—"

"Have you thought what you'll do?"

Vladimir strode down the trail overlooking the harbor and mediated by the water. He closed his eyes, imagining how peaceful life could be while Constantine continued to lecture him. "I don't know. Maybe do what normal people do: have kids, a family." Contemplating how he could disappear, he picked up a pebble on the ground and tossed it, watching as it bounced.

"Oh, no," Constantine exclaimed. "Don't tell me you've fallen in love with this woman."

Acting upon impulse, he ditched the phone into the water, never looking back as he ran as fast as he could.

***

Dana slid her hand on the satin sheets and peeked to see if Gio was still asleep, but instead, she found a note.

Went for a run. Get dressed. Want to take you somewhere nice.

A warm sensation tingled inside of her. Gio was full of surprises. After slipping out of bed, she hopped into the shower and allowed the hot water to lather her body. There were decisions she needed to make and no matter how much she weighed them out, Dana knew she couldn't imagine what life would be without Gio. She hoped this wasn't some kind of whirlwind romance that ended in a disaster. Even though she didn't know much about him, she knew enough to trust him.

Once she finished her shower, she toweled off and slipped into a satin robe. She applied lotion and moisturizer and combed and blow dried her hair. Forget her disguise. She wanted to look extra beautiful for Gio. Not Abigail Madison beautiful, but the Dana Simmons supermodel that she was.

Chapter 26

Vladimir dashed inside a phone shop and exhaled in relief when he was the only customer inside.

The clerk approached him. "Looking for a phone? We have the latest Samsung Gala–"

"Sure, I'll take that." He agreed.

"Great. Do you have an account with us?"

"I need a prepaid service. Won't be here for long."

The clerk circled around the counter and handed him the pre-paid card. "How are you liking Austin so far?" He assisted Vladimir with the phone.

"Love it."

"That's what everybody says." He giggled, covering his mouth as his gaze darted back and forth to Gio. "So, do you know how to do this?" he asked, ringing up the charges.

Gio took the bag from him. "Yes, thanks for your help."

"Have a great day."

Gio exited the shop and walked a few feet down the road so he could be alone. He scratched the card and plugged in all the info then made a phone call. Shivering, he turned around to see if there was anybody nearby. Then he cocked his head and transferred the phone to his right ear.

A sleepy voice picked up after four rings. "Hello."

"Courtney, it's me. Gio."

"Gio." She paused. "How's it going?" She yawned.

"Listen, I need you to do me a big favor."

"Anything for you. You made my dream come true."

"You're aware that your agent is in jail."

"Rob?"

"Don't you watch the news? Anyway, I'm going to text you instructions on what to do, but you're to tell nobody I sent you."

"Wait? What is going on?"

"Just wait for my text." Gio hung up. If he needed to make things right for Dana, he needed someone on his side to help him and Courtney would do it.

***

Stanley's squeaky shoes woke Rob from his sleep inside the jail cell. He had been dreaming of Dana and knew she was still alive and his exasperation and fear kept him awake at night. He was surprised to see a guard there.

"Rob Hanson, you're free to go." The guard opened the cell.

Rob beamed in delight. "Really?" Facing Stanley, he asked, "How did you get the bail money?"

"No bail was needed, but let's discuss more in my office about the findings," Stanley said.

Rob furrowed his eyebrows and followed the guard who escorted him to the front to retain his belongings.

"There are people outside ready to pounce on you. Please keep a straight face and answer no questions." Stanley kept Rob within arm's length.

A stream of reporters paraded themselves around him as soon as they exited.

"Mr. Hanson, what do you have to say about the murder of Stacy Kestav? Did you kill her?"

A splurge of anger burned within him. Rob could feel his face flushed. He struggled to maintain composure.

"Mr. Hanson, is it true that you blackmailed the models to have sex with you in the hope of building a successful career?"

Rob gasped, but Stanley squeezed his arm and faced the crowd. "My client is not answering any questions. Please respect his privacy."

A reporter sneaked in from of them and positioned the microphone in front of Rob. "Is it true that Stacy Kestav is dead because she threatened to expose you?"

Rob drew in an exasperated breath. "For the record, I am no murderer."

Stanley pushed him inside a black Cadillac. "Weren't my instructions clear?"

With head bowed down, Rob moaned. "I'm sorry, I can't believe they would say such horrible things."

"Trust me. Scandals sell."

"I don't understand. How'd you get me out?" Rob asked, fastening his seat belt.

Stepping on the gas, Stanley flashed him a grin. "It turns out that Stacy's father was in the pornography business."

"Oh my God!"

"Her sister discovered it in their basement. She phoned the FBI agents, and they came in with a warrant. They found the knife with a trace of blood and it matched Mr. Kestav's DNA as well as Stacy's."

"That's sick," Rob said, then coughed. "How could he kill his own daughter?"

"I know, but at least they found evidence and you're a free man."

Rob kept his gaze glued to the road and scratched his head. "Something's not right here. If the Kestav family is involved in the pornography business, they might know where Dana and her mother are."

"Will you get a grip on yourself and stop playing detective for once?"

His lips formed a hard line. "I need to speak with Agent Wayne and tell them what I found."

Swerving to the left, Stanley glared at him. "You need to stop, Rob. Aren't you happy you're not in jail anymore?"

"I don't think the Kestav family is alone in this business. This is bigger than you think. They need to find Michael Downey. Once they find him, they'll get answers."

***

Grinning from cheek to cheek, Dana stepped outside the bathroom and walked into Gio's bedroom. She felt her face flushed with excitement as she plucked a white polo shirt and dressed up. Then she slipped on the jeans she had on the hanger and her sandals. Overhearing the door close, she called out, "You're back."

Dana dashed outside to greet him... only a tall woman with long black hair and olive-toned skin stood by the door wearing a skimpy white dress with no bra. She tilted her head and smiled. "You don't look like the other women. The last one he had didn't stop chewing gum. She tasted good though."

A knot formed in her stomach. "I'm sorry, but are you a friend of Gio's?"

"Oh." She raised her eyebrows. "He didn't tell you." She fingered his silk shirts.

"Tell me what?" Heat enclosed her body, and her breathing became more rapid.

Approaching Dana, the woman twirled her hair. "Your man loves to play. I'm Amy, btw."

Taking a step back, Dana cleared her throat. "I need to go."

Gesturing her hands in the air, Amy pouted. "Gio's going to be sad you left before the party started."

Dana grabbed her purse and stormed out, heading for the elevator. Tears trickled down her cheeks. *How dare he!* She had trusted him when her instincts told her not to. She had been about to tell him everything. She hated *him*. She hated her *life*. She hated being alone *again*.

U.S. Marshall Collins was right. She couldn't trust anyone. Everyone she trusted betrayed her. But she had a mission to fulfill and everything ended here. She could no longer be Abigail Madison. She was going to find her mother and kill

Vladimir. No more distractions. Walking toward the harbor, she flung the cell phone U.S. Marshall Collins gave her in the water and fled. Dana knew where she needed to go.

***

Vladimir dashed inside his unit, breathless. "Abigail, I have exciting news to share with you." He strode to the bedroom and stopped in his tracks. A dark-haired woman lay underneath the bed sheets. "Who are you? Where's Abigail?"

The woman pushed the sheets down, revealing her naked body. "Oh, that scared shitless woman?" She gave a sly grin. "She left in such a hurry."

Vladimir picked up a vase on the dresser and threw it against the wall. "Please leave," he growled.

Rising from the bed, the woman grabbed her clothes. "Gladly." Covering her body, she added, "Constantine said you were fun to be with and liked adventure. It's too bad. I would have really liked to do you and your friend." She shrugged, heading toward the door before flashing him one last look. "Your loss."

Taking deep breaths, Vladimir felt a sharp pain in his palm. He spotted a piece of glass from the vase pressing against his skin. "Fuck." Vladimir fled to the kitchen and washed his hands. He plucked a towel and wrapped around his hand.

Clanking heels and the door shut were the last thing he heard before his landline rang. After five rings, there was a voicemail from Constantine.

Don't think you can get away from me, I'll come find you and when I do… You'll regret it.

Vladimir tugged the cord and smashed the phone. Staring at the night table, he noticed Dana left her locket. Opening, the necklace, he caught sight of the family photo with a young Dana. His heart sank. He would end this nightmare of a life and not live the life his father and Constantine wanted. Depositing the locket inside his pocket, he grabbed his keys and stormed out of the building. Today he will live his life the way he wanted it to be.

Chapter 27

U.S. Marshalls Collins and Adams surveyed Dana's house in Texas.

"Everything seems to be normal," U.S. Marshall Collins called out to his partner while eyeing the vegetables and fruits inside her refrigerator. "She has food to last her all week."

U.S. Marshall Collins appeared from the bedroom. "She left all her clothes and shoes intact."

"Where would she go? It's only been twenty-four hours, and she's supposed to work tomorrow."

U.S. Marshall Collins rubbed his chin. "Cara mentioned she had a new assistant. Good looking fellow, she said. Gio something.

"Why didn't Dana inform us about this? What happened to Courtney?"

"Moved to New York to be a model." He paused. "Wait a minute."

"We need to find Gio." U.S. Marshall Adams pulled out his cell phone.

"Before we do that, we need to tip the press that Dana Simmons is now dead."

***

Using his binoculars, Vladimir waited and watched the two men wearing clad-suits leave Dana's house. He knew these were the two U.S. Marshalls who protected her. If they couldn't find Dana, they would be looking for him. But where would Dana go?

After the U.S. Marshalls were nowhere in sight, Vladimir stepped out of his car and checked to see if anybody was watching. He put on his leather motorcycle gloves and headed for the back. Smashing the glass door with a rock, he slipped inside Dana's house hoping to find clues. He dug his hand underneath the couch. Nothing. Marching to her bedroom, he touched the sheets and underneath the mattress for any clues, but no luck. In the bathroom, Vladimir inspected her medicine cabinet and aside from Tylenol and a shaver, there was nothing there.

Back at the bedroom, he turned on the TV to watch the news, and a photo of Mr. Kestav flashed on the screen. The reporter announced how he had brutally murdered his daughter. Then they showed Rob Hanson coming out of jail. *I need to call Courtney.*

Without hesitation, he lifted the toilet bowl lid and discovered an envelope. "Bingo." He picked it up and went to the bedroom to sort its contents— photo of her parents, a magazine photo of Dana, and a ripped out folded calendar. He flipped the calendar and spotted only one thing scribbled in August. *Kill Vladimir Marcovic.*

His heart sank. *I need to find her*

After pacing the room back and forth, Vladimir raised his hand in the air. *New York.*

He texted Courtney instructions hoping to make things right for Dana.

***

At the station, FBI Agents Kerry and Felicia stood, watching the TV as photos of Dana Simmons flashed on the screen. The newscaster relayed how the supermodel's car skidded off the cliff and exploded in France.

"Now the whole world will believe she had a tragic death," Kerry said. "Such a waste. She was young, beautiful and had a whole life ahead of her."

"You're right, Rob Hanson should be here in a few minutes," Felicia said eyeing the clock. "I feel bad that he will be mourning Dana's loss."

Rob and his lawyer arrived at their office. Kerry cringed when she heard the squeaky shoes.

They all took their seats.

Stanley rolled up his sleeves and loosened his tie. "Rob believes there's more than just the pornography business." He gestured for Rob to continue.

Dehydrated looking, Rob relayed about the photos he discovered. "I believe this is a crime of human trafficking, and I'm positive Dana isn't dead."

The agents listened intently while Rob continued to provide information.

"We need to investigate further. Why would Michael Downey have a photo of Stacy Kestav?" Kerry asked.

Felicia swayed her hands. "You need to leave the investigating to us, Rob. Take a break. You just got out of jail. You need to lie low."

Rob growled. "I *need* to see Dana, I know she's coming home. She's not dead and there was no accident. Why the fuck can't you believe that! She has to know that I never stopped searching for her."

Agent Wayne appeased him. "Please, Mr. Hanson. From now on, let us do the rest. We'll notify you of any updates."

***

The bus screeched its tires to a full stop. Hiding in a hooded top and sweats, Dana stepped off the bus. She drew in the cool, fresh Alaskan air and bowed her head as she marched down the street. It would take her a half hour to get to the motel, but the walk would give her time to strategize her next step. What would she do once she met Michael Downey?

She didn't doubt that U.S. Marshall Collins and Adams would soon figure out where she is.. *This is judgment day. This has to end now.*

Her strides lengthened as thoughts of Gio flashed through Dana's mind. How could she be so naive? She had trusted him and saw a bright future together. But she hardly knew Gio, and he seemed that he could buy anything he wanted. He had power. And with power came ego, and ego could lead to destruction. Yet, she never anticipated he needed that for his *ego*.

Her thoughts shifted to her best friend, Rob. Was he looking for her? Did he actually believe the news that she saw this morning about her car accident? She knew the feelings she felt for Rob were not as intense as what she felt for Gio. Why did she have to let herself go?

***

Vladimir closed the curtain of his house and spread his numerous passports on the table. He was tired of living a double life. No more Gio Amorosi, Michael Downey, and the rest of his aliases. It was time he told the Feds the truth, that he was Vladimir Marcovic. Enough is enough. All he longed for was to have a normal family, now that he had met Dana.

He prepared all the information he needed to give to the Feds and sat on his desk. Vladimir hoped his instructions to Courtney were clear and all he needed to do was wait. Eyeing the calendar, he grinned. Today was the first day of August—the month Dana planned to kill him.

Chapter 28

After meeting with the FBI agents, Rob stepped in the cab and joined Courtney."What's so important that you couldn't tell me over the phone?"

Courtney gave the cab instructions then turned toward Rob "There's so much to tell you."

"So, *tell* me."

She passed Rob her iPhone where a long email was displayed.

Using his fingers, Rob zoomed the screen and read.

> *Dear Courtney,*
>
> *What I'm about to tell you might come as a shock to you. My real name is not Gio Amorosi. I've used many aliases over the years, but I only have one name and that's Vladimir Marcovic. I'm not proud of my disguise and for the things I've done, but I'm here to make it right.*
>
> *You see, Courtney, it was no accident why we met. I came to your*

store to meet your manager, Abigail Madison, who also carries an alias. Abigail Madison is actually Dana Simmons—yes, Dana Simmons the supermodel. Dana and I share one thing in common—a father. Her biological dad is my adoptive father. My father was the leader of the Russian mob, which still exists now since he passed the business to me. Dana's mother was my father's mistress, but she left him when she saw that he was involved in human trafficking.

I'm ashamed of all the filthy things our family has done, but I stuck it out to honor my father's last request. He asked me to find Dana's mother and his daughter Dana. His last words were to protect them. Anger and guilt have consumed me since I promised him that I will find them, so instead of protecting them, I planned to kill them both.

I was this close to killing Dana, but my heart got the better part of me. She's a beautiful woman inside and out, and as fate would have it, I fell in love with her. With Dana, all I saw was beauty and I was oblivious to the cruel world around us. I thought I could run away from it all and take her with me, but being tied to the mob, they're now after me. Dana doesn't know yet that

Gio and Vladimir are the same person. She has set out to kill me.

Since I want to make this right, show this letter to Rob Hanson. I know he hasn't stopped searching for Dana and will cooperate with you. You need to take Dana's mother to Dana's apartment in Manhattan right away. I know Dana will be waiting for her. I will text you the address from a separate number.

I hope you do this for me, Courtney, and I thank you for everything.

Vladimir

Taking a deep breath, Rob turned to Courtney. "I don't know what to say. I can't believe this. This man is responsible for everything. His family destroyed Dana's life."

"I know, but we don't have time to think about that now. We have to do this quick."

The cab screeched to a curb in front of a tall glass building, and Courtney handed the cabbie folded bills as they stepped out.

"Now, here's the drill." She wrapped her arm around Rob's. "You're my husband, and we wanted to try something new in the bedroom."

"Okay, Aileen Williams," he said to play along as they entered the building and approached the elevator.

Courtney pressed the button and straightened her skirt. "Let me fix your tie, Josh."

The elevator opened, and they walked through the front desk.

A man greeted them. "How can I help you?"

Twirling her hair, Courtney approached him while Rob stayed behind, studying the murals on the wall. "Hi, I'm Aileen and, um, my husband and I are having trouble in the bedroom lately," she whispered."And I was wondering if…" She covered her face with her hand. "If we can get a woman who can spice things up. You know, that type of thing."

The man beamed. "Oh, I hear you. I think our ladies will know what to do."

"Really?" Courtney grinned with excitement. "We need somebody younger than me, probably with dark hair." She mumbled, "He's tired of blonds."

The man nodded and picked up a folder. "Would you like to look at the selection?"

"Sure." Courtney took the folder and turned to Rob. "Honey, help me choose."

The man cleared his throat. "Would you like any of our themed rooms? We have everything from Cinderella to safari or water themes."

"Hmm, that's interesting," Rob said. "Do you have a room closer to the ground?" He eyed Courtney. "I have fear of heights."

"But of course." The man smiled. "That would be the under the sea theme."

"Cool," Rob said.

"Why don't you have a seat while you choose. Would you like a drink while you wait?"

Collapsing on the couch, Rob loosened his tie. "How about you send champagne to our room and make sure it's chilled."

"Very well. Let me excuse myself."

Courtney waited until he was out of earshot to whisper, "Okay, while I stay in the room, you get Marcy. When they bring in the girl, I'll say you're in the bathroom." She hands him a key. "There's a black Honda Civic at the back of the building. It's tinted. Just give me a missed call once you've escaped, and I'll make one quick phone call to the FBI."

He tucked the key into his pocket. "You're sure you'll be okay?"

She squeezed his hand. "Don't worry about me. I can tell them you chickened out."

"Thank you." He paused. "And to think I always pass by this building and never anticipated this."

Courtney cleared her throat as the man arrived.

"Champagne has been sent to your room. Here are two keys. Have you made your selection?"

"Yes." Courtney rose from the couch and pointed to their choice. "We both agreed that she looks like a doll."

"Good pick. I'll bring her right upstairs in, say, five minutes?"

"We'll be waiting." Courtney winked then held Rob's hand as they strode down the hallway. "Take my purse with you. I have two wigs and sunglasses. The password for the lock is three-one-three. Get the hell out of here. Hurry."

Rob nodded and fled to the elevator.

***

Lying down in bed, Marcy closed her eyes. With Stacy gone, she had nobody to talked too.

Days were a routine, and her hope dwindled. *Will I ever see my daughter again?*

Just then, she heard the door unlock.

A tall man she never saw before stepped inside. With dark hair, he wore a suit and carried a woman's purse.

"Marcy Simmons, I'm a friend of your daughter. There's no time to explain." He opened the purse and tossed her a wig and sunglasses while he put on his. "You need to come with me."

She flinched. "How sure am I you're telling me the truth?"

"Let me explain in the car. Let's go." The world was spinning fast and Marcy couldn't process what was going on.

Chapter 29

U.S. Marshall Collins and Adams stepped out of the car. FBI agents Wayne and Raymond greeted them outside the building with their team.

"Thanks for cooperating with us on this matter," U.S. Marshall Collins said. "We still haven't found Dana."

"We have your back," Kerry said. "And we won't leave until we find her."

"As you know, the agent who handled Anton Marcovic's case has been trying to catch the mob for ages," Kerry chimed in. "Each time we raid a warehouse filled with teenage Russian prostitutes, another one opens. They've been very good at covering their tracks."

"I know," U.S. Marshall Adams said. "Their family is scattered all over the state. They have blended in to look like normal businessmen with legitimate companies to cover up their illegal business."

"So, what is the protocol?" Felicia raised her eyebrows. "Even if we invade this building, and catch them, what makes us believe they don't have counterparts in other states? This is a never-ending goose chase."

U.S. Marshall Adams removed a folder from his bag and handed it to Felicia. "Constantine, Vladimir's cousin, who seems to be the notorious one. And there's six other cousins who take orders from both Vladimir and Constantine."

"What about their wives and kids?" Kerry asked. "They could also be involved."

"We're going to target the leaders and hope to bring down the business."

"That doesn't erase the human trafficking problem that goes on every day," Felicia said, averting her gaze to the building.

"You're right, but like you, we are here to protect the innocent from the wicked. Each time you solve a crime or put the bad guys away, you get to appreciate your job more and sleep peacefully at night knowing you made a difference," U.S. Marshall Collins said.

"So are we ready?" Kerry asked.

The FBI agents, U.S. Marshalls, and their teams barged in the building wearing their bullet-proof vests and carrying their weapons. A number of them marched down the stairs to the basement while the rest took the elevator to the third floor.

For the first time in his life, Kerry felt afraid. He couldn't bare the sight of seeing teenage girls suffering. After this case was over, he would take a vacation to visit his daughters.

***

Constantine knocked on room one-hundred, wondering why the couple who requested one of their girls and rented the room for two hours hadn't check out yet.

"Is everything okay?" he called.

No answer.

He unlocked the door, gently opened it, and squinted his eyes in the dark room. "Shit, where are they?"

Turning on the switch, he noticed the room had been untouched. Dashing to the bathroom, he found, *We caught you now* in red lipstick displayed on the mirror.

"Shit." He skipped outside and bumped into four armed men wearing masks.

"Constantine Marcovic, you're under arrest. You have the right to remain silent." They handcuffed him and continued to state his rights.

Cries of outrage from down below overwhelmed him as they pulled him. Men were running out of their rooms naked while the FBI raided the building.

"You need to tell us where the others are."

He didn't say a word.

"Where is Marcy Simmons?"

"She should be in her room, third floor."

"We checked every room and she's not there."

"That's impossible. How could she escape?" He paused, gathering his thoughts. "Vladimir must have done this."

"Where is Vladimir?"

Constantine grinned. "Why should I tell you?"

***

Later that evening, washed out FBI agents and U.S. Marshalls stayed inside the conference room.

"I want to thank you both for all the effort you've put in this case. We couldn't have done it without you," U.S. Marshall Collins said with conviction.

"We still haven't caught Vladimir," Felicia said.

"That's correct, but we rescued more than a hundred teenagers and I've made calls to an organization that can help these women rebuild their lives," Kerry said.

"Guys, we've done enough for the day. Let's discuss more tomorrow," U.S. Marshall Adams added.

U.S. Marshall Collins turned the TV to the news. Constantine and the Marcovic family were handcuffed and dragged inside a van by the FBI. A female reporter relayed the story. "Today is a day of celebration and misery. The Marcovic clan, a Russian mob involved in human trafficking has been caught." The tall glass building in Manhattan was displayed. "Who would think this building was a prison for these Russian girls who were forced to be prostitutes? These innocent woman were drugged, raped, and abused. We celebrate their freedom today."

The camera turned to teenage Russian girls weeping and embracing each other.

"But the saga continues while the FBI is in hunt for the leader of this group, Vladimir Marcovic who seems to have disappeared. We also have been tipped from our anchorwoman, Jenny Wang that supermodel Dana Simmons is very much alive. Jenny, take the lead."

U.S. Marshall Adams turned the volume up.

"Thank you, Tricia, lots of news going on today," Jenny said. "I received a video a few minutes ago from Dana Simmons, and she has a message to Vladimir Marcovic."

The screen showed Dana dressed in a white shirt and jeans She gazed at the camera and didn't bat her eyelashes. "Vladimir Marcovic, I know you've been looking for me. I'm tired of running away and hiding so I ask that you come see me tomorrow afternoon at three at my Manhattan apartment. You know where I live, and I hope you show up."

Turning off the TV, U.S. Marshall Collins addresses to his partner and FBI agents, "Let's go."

Chapter 30

Dana Simmons stood outside her childhood home in Anchorage, Alaska. While the rest of the world thought she'd be back in Manhattan, she had taken a step further wanting to be ahead. If Vladimir knew how to play the game, so did she. A cold shiver ran through her spine as memories of her father flooded her. His last wish was for Dana to find her mother, and Dana would after she killed Vladimir Marcovic.

A grin played on her face as she inserted her hand inside her pocket for the Colt .45 she purchased earlier today with her Lucy Mitchell ID along with a silencer. Although she bought a stack of bullets, she only needed one bullet to kill the *motherfucker.* And if she died today… She averted her gaze to the clouds and shook her head. *There's no option. I'm going to live.*

A chilly mist blew against her as she zipped up her hood and stepped in the driveway.

***

U.S. Marshall Collins and Adams, together with FBI agents Wayne and Raymond, surrounded the perimeter of Dana Simmons's Manhattan apartment. A group of reporters blocked the driveway as passersby inched their way to get a closer look.

"I don't know why she had to announce her plans on national TV," Kerry remarked.

Felicia chewed on her nail. "Something's not right."

"Don't tell me you have another hunch?" Kerry asked.

"Like you said, why would she want to announce her plans on national TV?"

U.S. Marshall Collins eyed his watch. "It's time. We need to go upstairs."

***

Marcy and Rob waited outside Dana's apartment after knocking.

"Are you sure I'm going to see my daughter again?" Marcy wiped tears from her eyes. She couldn't believe the series of events that happened, but all she ever wished for was to see her daughter again.

Three men and a lady approached.

Marcy froze.

"Marcy Simmons," U.S. Marshall Collins said. "You're alive. And you must be Rob Hanson."

Rob shook hands with the U.S. Marshalls and turned to FBI agents Wayne and Raymond as he relayed what happened and showed them the letter from Vladimir.

Marcy shared with them about how she was locked up in a room with no windows and the time she spent with Stacy. "I never thought I would come out of this alive, but Rob saved me."

Agent Wayne opened Dana's apartment using the key the manager had given him earlier. The group followed him.

"Nothing's changed since she left," Rob said, studying the living room.

"How are we going to handle this?" Marcy asked. "Do you think Vladimir will show up as well? What if he kills us all?"

***

Skinny as she was, Dana managed to slip through the back window inside the house. What would she tell Michael Downey when she saw him? Could he protect her from Vladimir? This was the only place she could find refuge while the whole world thought she was back at her Manhattan apartment. She froze as she noticed the white space and black and white paintings on the wall. The popcorn ceilings and wallpaper were gone, and everything about the house was a complete replica of her Manhattan apartment.

Inching her way to the kitchen, Dana opened the refrigerator, but it was empty. The kitchen was spotless, and the furniture looked like they were used to stage the house. Nothing about it spelled home, erasing the memories she once had.

She was about to go upstairs when she heard humming from the basement. Footsteps drew closer. Running to the corner, she ducked.

***

Felicia stared outside the window of Dana's apartment. The crowd had increased, and still there were no signs of Dana. "She's not coming."

Agent Wayne pulled out a stool. "Relax. It's only been three minutes."

"She's right," Rob chimed in. "Dana would never do such a thing unless she had a different agenda. Although she graced the limelight, when it comes to her personal life, Dana was very private."

"We can't just sit here and speculate," U.S. Marshall Collins interjected.

"I know where she is," Marcy spoke in a hushed tone.

All eyes turned to her.

"Alaska."

***

The humming grew louder than the footsteps. From the hiding spot, Dana glanced at the mirror on the wall. Her body grew limp as she saw the reflection of the one person she never thought she'd see.

Catching her breath, she felt like her heart had been ripped out to pieces. *Gio is Michael Downey?* She heard him walking back and forth, dumping boxes on the floor. *Why is he packing?*

And then it dawned on her. There was no Gio nor Michael. A knot formed in her stomach. She had been sleeping with the enemy all along. He had played her from the very start.

She reached inside her pocket. *This could end now with just one shot.*

***

Vladimir dumped the last box in the corner and was about to leave when he took one last look of the house he bought last December. Tomorrow, it would be just a faded memory as he began a new life free from the mob. He would turn himself in to the Feds, but first he needed to find Dana and let her know he was a new man.

He reached into his pocket and pulled out the locket she left on his nightstand in Austin.

"Are you looking for me?" A female voice startled him.

As he turned around, he saw Dana pointing a gun right before him.

Their eyes locked. He didn't say a word as he watched her standing like a statue, never failing to blink.

"So this is where it all ends, Vladimir."

Vladimir wanted to confess everything to Dana and tell her that he was ready to come clean with the Feds, but he seemed to have lost his tongue as she lashed out at him.

"How could you live this way knowing you've destroyed people's lives—my life! How can you sleep at night?"

He didn't lose her gaze knowing Dana believed what a cold-hearted psychopath he was.

"I lost my mother because of you. Your father destroyed my life."

He wanted to tell her that their father destroyed his, but he continued to bite his tongue. This was Dana's moment, and if she wanted to kill him, he would die peacefully knowing he gave Dana her wish.

She took a step forward. Her body shook as she burst into tears. "Please say something."

His heart told him to embrace her, but he couldn't, wouldn't. He just stood still watching her—obsessed, oblivious like nobody existed.

He witnessed the rage and anger tore upon her as she yelled like an animal, her hand almost pulling the trigger. "God damn it. Why can't I shoot you?"

He straightened his shoulders. "I will never force you to do anything you don't want to. If you kill me today, it will be a choice you will need to live with for the rest of your life. Only you can decide if that's the right choice."

Her face grew pale, allowing him to see the vulnerable Dana he knew. There was so much love beyond that rage. Although he hated his past, their circumstances brought them together.

Dana put her hands down. "I'm going to count to five. If you don't get out of here, I'll shoot you."

He blinked, but she wasn't looking at him.

"One." She sighed. "Two."

Tucking in the locket, he pulled out his gun and pointed it at her. "Three."

**

Dana flinched as Vladimir aimed his gun at her. And here she thought she had the upper hand.

Cocking the Colt .45, she said, "Four."

"Five."

"Six." She approached him.

"Seven." He pointed at her heart.

It was a matter of time that they both would kill each other. Heart pounding, muscles tensing, and palms sweating, there was no way she could shoot him. She was positive he had killed women before, so what would stop him from killing her? She had to delay this.

"Since we're going to both die, do you have any last words you want to tell me?"

He bit his lip then looked her in the eye with no remorse. "From the moment my father told me about you, I promised myself I'd find you and kill you."

She stared at him, dumbfounded. The sweet Gio she had shared her dreams with was a monster. She had to kill him.

"Eight." He grinned. "Do you have any last words for me?"

She had to think fast. Memories of her parents flashed through her mind on the eve of her birthday when her mother vanished. Tears flooded her vision as she felt like the helpless ten-year-old girl she was when she lost her mother. She had never allowed herself to grieve all these years.

While she choked upon tears, her legs wobbled and her vision became blurry and the next thing she knew, she collapsed on the floor and everything went black.

***

All Vladimir wanted to do was embrace Dana and tell her how much he loved her and how sorry he was for all the pain she had gone through, but it was too late. It was better this way. He would start somewhere new. All that mattered now was for Dana and her mother to be together again. He carried her to the back of the house and up to the tree house. As she slept like a baby, he leaned close and softly kissed her, tasting the sweetness of her lips. *I love you, Dana.*

***

Ten hours later, Marcy and Rob dashed into the Alaskan home as the U.S. Marshalls trailed behind them.

"Dana." Marcy checked the rooms.

"No sign of her," Rob said.

"I'll check the basement," U.S. Marshall Collins said.

They followed him downstairs. As he turned on the light, they spotted passports and documents lying on the floor with a note.

Agent Collins read it aloud:

> *To the Feds who have been searching for me,*
> *Everything you need is on this list. This is where it ends. I ask that you stop looking for me. From time to time, you may receive an anonymous tip, and you'll know it's from me.*
> *V*

U.S. Marshall Collins tucked the documents inside his messenger bag.

"I know where she is." Marcy headed to the back door while they followed her.

They strode to the tree house Marcy climbed up, and her heart melted as she saw her daughter open her eyes.

"Mom?"

"I'm home, sweetie. I'm home."

Dana smiled. "I never got to tell you what Dad said."

Marcy stroked Dana's cheek.

"He told me to find you and when I did," she paused. "He said to tell you he never stopped loving you."

Tears spilled from Marcy's eyes. "I'm never leaving you again, Dana."

Epilogue

One year later

Dana arranged the scarves on the counter as Rob popped in Dana Simmons' Shop.

"Surprise!" He kissed her.

"You weren't joking when you mentioned you'll be spending Christmas with us," Dana wiped her tears. Rob had been her loyal friend till the end. What would she do without him?

Marcy came in through the back door. "I told him Christmas is better here in Alaska."

"Well, if you can't come to New York, I might as well spend Christmas with my two favorite people." He embraced them both.

"Let me close the register while you two catch up," Marcy said.

"I'm so happy you're here." Dana faced Rob.

Rob pulled out a stool and sat down. "Me too, but you could always move back."

"Nah." Dana smiled. "I thought I'd never move here, but Alaska seems to have worked its charm on me."

He grinned. "Oh, by the way, this was pasted on the door." Rob handed her an envelope with her name.

"I wonder who it's from." She opened it and removed a card. A locket fell into her hands. She froze as she read the letter.

Dear Dana,

I believe this locket belongs to you. I'm sorry I kept it with me. I thought by keeping it, you would remain close to me. I see that you're happy now and have made a life for yourself. I never got to tell you what my actual last words for you were, so here it is: I can never imagine life without you, but I have to live with that choice every day. Just knowing that you're safe and happy reduces every bit of pain I have. I love you, Dana. I will never forget you. Thank you for sharing a piece of you with me.

V

Dana held the locket and card close to her chest as tears spilled from her eyes.

"Are you okay? Who is that from?" Rob asked.

She sniffed. "It's from an old friend." She lifted her hair and put the necklace around her neck then stared outside the window, wondering what tomorrow might bring her.

Acknowledgements

A heartfelt thanks to the following people who have made Never Look Back possible:

1. Editor, Nicole Zoltack for your keen eye and thorough edits of my manuscript.

2. Proofreader, Gail Picado who pointed out things I overlooked and kept my story consistent.

3. Cover artist, Natasha Brown for the amazing cover you created. I'm still so dazzled by it.

4. Formatter, Rachelle Ayala for your professionalism and friendship.

5. Contra Costa County Deputy Sheriffs Association President, Ken Westermann for assisting me with my research of the Witness Protection program and for providing good insight.

6. And to my beloved son and supportive husband who perfectly understood why I had to work everyday till the wee hours to complete this novel. You are both my greatest treasures.

ABOUT THE AUTHOR

Geraldine Solon is the award-winning, best-selling author of five novels and a marketing guidebook for authors. Two of her books have been adapted into film. Geraldine was awarded as a *Modern Day Hero* by the Philippine Consul General in San Francisco for her numerous and significant contributions to Filipino American art and culture. She served as Treasurer, Event Coordinator and Vice President for the Fremont Area Writers club and is the Executive Producer of her upcoming movie, Love Letters.